Unveiling Love

A London Regency Suspense Tale:
Episode I

Vanessa Riley

Books by Vanessa Riley

Madeline's Protector

Swept Away, A Regency Fairy Tale

The Bargain, A Port Elizabeth Tale, Episodes I-IV

Unveiling Love, Episodes I-IV

Unmasked Heart, A Regency Challenge of the Soul Series

Sign up at VanessaRiley.com for contests, early releases, and more.

Copyright © 2016 Vanessa Riley

Published by BM Books

A Division of Gallium Books

Suite 236B, Atlanta, GA 30308

ISBN-13: 978-1-943885-08-4

SAVING A MARRIAGE OR WINNING THE TRIAL OF THE CENTURY

Dear Lovely Reader,

Unveiling Love is a serialized historical romance or soap opera told in episodes. Each episode averages three to eight chapters, about 18,000 to 30,000 words. Each episode resolves one issue. Emotional cliffhangers may be offered, but the plot, the action of the episode, will be complete in resolving this issue.

My promise to you is that the action will be compelling, the romance passionate, and the journey like nothing you've read before. I will tell you in the forward the length. This episode, Episode I, is eight chapters long, 30,000 words. Enjoy this Regency Romance.

Vanessa Riley

Winning in the courts, vanquishing England's foes on the battlefield, Barrington Norton has used these winner-take-all rules to script his life, but is London's most distinguished mulatto barrister prepared to win the ultimate fight, restoring his wife's love?

Amora Norton is running out of time. The shadows in her mind, which threaten her sanity and alienate Barrington's love, have returned. How many others will die if she can't piece together her shattered memories? Can she trust that Barrington's new found care is about saving their marriage rather than winning the trial of the century?

This is the first Regency Romance of four episodes.

Sign up for my newsletter at www.vanessariley.com or www.christianregency.com. Notices of releases, contests, my Regency Lover's pack, and other goodies will be made available to you.

Dedication

I dedicate this book to my copy editor supreme, my mother, Louise, my loving hubby, Frank, and my daughter, Ellen. Their patience and support have meant the world to me.

I also dedicate this labor of love to critique partners extraordinaire: June, Mildred, Lori, Connie, Gail.

Love to my mentor, Laurie Alice, for answering all my endless questions.

Love to Sharon & Kathy, they made me feel the emotion. You're never second place in my heart.

And I am grateful for my team of encouragers: Sandra, Michela, Felicia, Piper, and Rhonda.

CAST OF PRIMARY CHARACTERS

Barrington Norton: a barrister by trade, he is a free-borne mulatto gentleman of a wealthy black merchant's daughter and a landowner's ne'er-do-well son.

Amora Norton: the wife of Barrington Norton. She is of mixed blood, the daughter of an Egyptian woman and a wealthy Spanish apple merchant.

Smith: a man convicted of coining.

Cynthia Miller: a songstress and sister of Gerald Miller.

Gerald Miller: Barrington's best friend who saved his life during the Peninsula War.

Mr. Beakes: Barrington's solicitor.

Vicar Wilson: a minister serving at St. Georges.

Duke and Duchess of Cheshire: the newly married William St. Landon and Gaia Telfair

Mrs. Gretling: an abigail to Amora.

James: a man-of-all-work to Barrington.

Mr. Charleton: a rival of Barrington from their youth.

Chapter One: London, England August 4, 1819

Barrington Norton loathed Newgate prison. The caustic smells, the cackles of the men driven mad awaiting release, the curses of the one's sentenced to die, many of whom he'd condemned — all churned his innards.

He popped off his top hat and fanned his face. Thinking and rethinking this visit twisted his resolve, tearing through his flesh like hot lead shots. Perhaps he should've headed home to his wife's fretful arms.

Hating indecision, he donned his hat again and climbed out of his carriage. He couldn't in good conscience forgo the opportunity to save an innocent life.

He shuttled toward the prison, away from his man-of-all-work. Good old James would slow him down offering wretched cockney wisdom. It was good to laugh. This just wasn't one of those days. Delay could antagonize Amora, shifting her into another of her strange moods, shooting a hole into all the good work he'd done these past months. He'd been on schedule, sent notes over the slightest changes. She seemed more at ease, more tolerant of his court work. That had to be good, even if he felt leashed.

The gaoler opened the massive door. "Barrister, what brings you here? Court finished hours ago. We're setting up the Debtor's Platform for tomorrow. Coming early for a good seat?"

"No. Spectators at an execution is reprehensible. Death is not a game for sport. I'm here to see Smith. Take me to him."

With a raised brow, the gaoler frowned then turned toward the long hall leading to the bowels of the prison. "This way, Mr. Norton. Smith's not on the list for tomorrow's ropes. Curious, ye wanting to see him."

Barrington followed. The sour scent of urine hit him, reminding him of years long past. Bad years. He pulled a cloth from his pocket and wiped his face, savoring the hint of lavender. Amora's fragrance. A symbol of their blooming love, of easier days.

Married for five years, engaged for three, things weren't the same as the day he spied her painting in the Tomàs Orchards. He wasn't the same either, changed by war and the positioning of London politics.

The gaoler stopped and unlocked an iron door. He stepped in front of Barrington. "Smith's in here. Mighty funny, ye trying to save the man ye convicted. Is that fickleness a custom for you people?"

Barrington glared at the man. He made his tone tight, a notch below menacing. "What do you mean my people? Did you mean mulattos or barristers?"

"Ah...I ugh, meant no disrespect. Barristers."

Barrington stepped around the gaoler. "Yes, that's what we barristers for the crown do. We fight for truth."

The fellow didn't retort with a more open slur. He shrugged and closed the cell behind Barrington as he went inside.

Smith lay on a small cot. He jerked up and raised his fists, storming towards Barrington. "Came to gloat?"

The words he'd struggled over still hadn't materialized. He coughed and stuffed the handkerchief back into his pocket.

"What do you want, barrister?" He lunged closer and shook his knuckles near Barrington's face. "Get out of here, you half-breed, before I darken your daylights."

Barrington didn't move, staring, daring him to strike. Every muscle strained, pulling tight, tight, tighter, burning all the way to the missing bullet in his hip. "You let yourself be convicted for coining. You let the runners charge you with counterfeiting money. You let the sentence fall, started to dispute it, then stopped. I need to know why you chose to die."

Smith lowered his hand. His jowls dropped. His eyes drifted to the left.

Barrington knew that regret-filled look. It shoved his gut from hot indignation to sweet winning. He hovered over Smith using his height to crowd and corner him against the block wall. "They're building the hanging platform for the morning's executions. Hear the hammering. Pound. Pound. P-OU-ND."

He mimicked the sound again, exaggerating the echo, as if it were Justice Burn's gavel knocking against his desk. "Your name is not on the list this time, but it will be in a month. Tell me what you are hiding, and I'll get the sentence re-examined. I am your one chance to live."

Smith pushed past him and sank onto the mattress. "I have friends. They're going to help me, not the man who put me here."

"Unless these friends come forward and confess, you will die. Die with the truth. Whoever made you look guilty will die laughing."

"You and your smooth words. They will save me? You're dressed for a fancy party, barrister. Take your top hat and go."

Slam. A board or the platform's trap door must've fallen outside. It might as well have been the bailiff shutting up the doors to the Old Bailey. Barrington lost the argument. He turned and almost pressed upon the cell bars. Instead, he fished in his pocket and dropped onto a rickety table a couple of leaves of a Psalm, pages taken from the Bible he took to war. "If you don't trust my words, here's something that can save you. If you change your mind, send for me. I'll come."

Smith didn't move.

This visit was hopeless. A waste of precious time, time meant for Amora. He knocked on the bars to be let out. There wasn't a blasted thing Barrington could do. An innocent man was going to hang.

Amora Norton waited for the servants to clear her dinner setting as she sat next to her husband in the grand ballroom of Lord and Lady Cheshire. The soft strain of the violin's concerto caressed her ear as nineteen men with poufy powdered wigs and shiny blue liveries made the plates laced with garlicky fish remnants disappear.

Tonight, no shaking dread, no shivers of isolation seized her lungs, just a small swish of joy swirled at her middle. The pressure that pricked her high in the stomach eased when she shifted to the left against the dark stiles of her chair. Still not quite pain free, she pushed back in her dinner chair only to have its scrolled feet squeal and announce her restlessness.

Her husband continued his conversation with the gentleman on the other side of the crisp white tablecloth. Thank goodness he hadn't noticed the noise. Disappointing Barrington would ruin everything.

He'd been late to arrive at Mayfair, their London residence, but still wished to drag her to this ball. A deep frown marred his face. The stewing in his grey eyes whispered he needed care. She'd give him that, and more.

This proud man was her world, her anchor in shadow-filled London. So Amora didn't question him. She made him his favorite tea, wore his favorite bland dress. By the last course, the smelly fish, his mood had lifted.

The sultry tone of the songstress, Cynthia Miller, floated in the air, the lyrics haunting, soulful, man-snaring. She must be exhibiting to catch some new lover as she'd done for the beaus in their small Clanville village.

"Amora. Amora, dear."

Wanting to pinch herself for dwelling on the tart and not her husband's tall form, she blinked and looked up at Barrington. "Yes?"

Barrington's hands covered hers.

Her breath stopped, then curled in her throat. "Yes, Barrington."

"You are so beautiful, Mrs. Norton."

Shyly-smiling, she caught his gaze, counted the slow rises of his chest. Could he see how hard she'd worked to be pleasing? "I want to be for you."

Like a slow, distant wave, the chairs were pushed away from the tables. A set formed. Would they dance?

Usually he'd go politic or leave Amora for time with his patroness. "Do you think the floor is chalked? Can you see over the crowd?"

"My dear, what if we find out? Do you feel well enough to dance?"

"Yes."

Her pulse ticked to the timing of the violins. She came to his side savoring the crisp smell of his bergamot soap. The scent hung about his broad shoulders, wrapping him with appeal that stole everything -- good-sense, decorum, and the desire to stay at this ball.

The lenses of his spectacles reflected the tall candelabras brightening the room. He tugged on his gloves. "Good, I wish to dance with the loveliest woman here."

Her cheeks heated. "After all this time, you still make me blush as if I wore pigtails."

She wished she'd stayed a hope-filled girl, not jaded, or tormented, or fear-laden.

Barrington cleared his face of wanting, that caress until dawn heat in his gaze. He must have remembered they were in a public place and reigned in his passions.

She winced, put her hand to her stomach, then told herself it was nothing. A man had no time for a sick wife. He definitely wouldn't share a bed with one. And she needed him to be with her, distracting and holding her. The nightmares had returned.

"Your gloves, my dear?"

"Gloves?" Oh, the boring beige things. Twisting her naked fingers, she pivoted and searched her seat. They were missing. "They were here, Barrington."

The young servant who had attended her came from the edges holding the fallen mitts. "Here, ma'am."

The young man, blonde with pretty eyes of airy azure helped her tug on the satin, one after the other. With that hair, the servant could be a grown-up version of the little miracle, the orphan she'd read to this morning at the Foundling Hospital.

"Ma'am, is there anything else you need?"

"No, but thank you." Before she could pivot to her husband, the poor boy coughed and swallowed hard.

Amora's heart melted as she observed the creases under his young eyes. He looked so tired. Working at these long balls required so much, and an event for the Duke of Cheshire introducing his new duchess, must consume even more.

Called to that need, Amora put her hand to her half-filled water goblet and started to lift it to the servant, but Barrington claimed Amora's elbow. "Now, we are ready for a proper dance."

Proper. Barrington's need to be above reproach. The desire to help slipped away in a useless sigh. "Of course."

She was here for Barrington, not to make a spectacle of herself acting out of station. What she wanted didn't matter anymore, never mattered, so she acquiesced to his gentle pull.

He led her to the center of the room and twirled her in the first motion of the reel.

Her husband looked handsome in his dark silken waistcoat with jingly silver buttons. The onyx jacket and pure white cravat covered his strong form. His gaze met hers, not looking over her head to find someone to ramble on about trials. But, this would end. It always ended, and she would be alone.

The set parted. His fingers stayed and lightly brushed her abdomen. His voice kissed her ear. He bent his tall frame closer. "Want some air?"

No, she wanted to leave and abandon the ball before something or someone stole his attention. Yet, a niggle of guilt swirled in her innards alongside his babe. *I should do more in public to benefit his career.* He so loved his career.

Borrowing some resiliency from the Egyptian kings within her bloodline, she reached for his cheek. "The Dowager Clanville is seated near the entrance. Go speak with your patroness. Her attention upon you will do more than mine. I've had you all evening."

His chin lifted then lowered as his nose wriggled beneath his silver frames. "I'll let her rakish son keep her company. Only you tonight."

Did he mean it? Her heart beat again, tapping faster and louder as his words penetrated her mind. "For me, it's always been you."

He dimpled. "Then to the balcony before Mr. Charleton presses this way and insists upon a dance."

Her husband was so fine-looking with his jet colored hair lightly winged with gray, his swarthy brown skin. Built to be a warrior, he fought for justice with everything in his soul. Yet, that zeal seemed to blind him to other's faults and many times his own worth. "You needn't be concerned of any other."

"Well, I have a wide jealous streak and a boring road cut down my middle. And you've been so wonderful, Amora, never flirting or entertaining rakes, even whilst I was away three years at war."

"You're dependable and strong."

If tonight and every day forward, he used that strength to protect their marriage, to protect her and this baby, maybe her joy might be full again.

The smile forming his lips could be no

better than one of his kisses. His hand brushed the tiny swell of her abdomen as he steered her through the mob. Three months of carrying his babe had changed things between them, in so many good ways. Knowing where Barrington was, that he was safe, and that he'd always come home to her also did her much good.

He danced her onto the balcony. One step, two. He spun her under the bright stars then held her, sweeping her to the bricked corner along the stone railing.

Barrington ran a thumb under her chin. "You are very patient to attend these tedious things with me. The Duke of Cheshire hinted at needing my assistance. Perhaps that is no longer the case."

A sigh left his full lips, surely kissed with disappointment.

"You have nothing to prove to the ton, to anyone."

He pushed up his slipping lenses. "I like proving things. I like winning even more. But you must be rewarded. What bauble may I procure? Say a locket for the babe's first curl?"

"I want nothing but your love. To know you love all of me." She wedged her hands beneath his tailcoat and roamed the solid muscles of his back. This moment was not a dream, not a waking vision. Things had finally meshed. After his baby was born, their marriage would grow strong, strong enough to survive anything, even her secrets.

"Do you think it's a boy? I think so. I want to be a good father, a good man like my grandfather."

He would be a good one like her own, nothing like his. She peered up, catching Barrington's delighted gaze. "In a little more than a half year, we'll know. But if it is a son, may he grow as tall as you."

In the soft light, she made out his grin, heard the music of his chuckles. "I've never complained of your height, or lack thereof. You are the right size for me. I can pick you up in one arm and shelter you. And you've such wondrous raven hair. Is it a gift from your Spanish side or the Egyptian? A gift none the less."

They were both of mixed blood. That had to be why they belonged together. And yet it had to be why it was so hard to survive in London. They were different than this place, sunshine and shade. Back in Clanville, where his grandfather and her father ruled, no one dared question their marriage. If only home were an option.

Her pulse raced as Barrington's lips anointed her wrist. "What say you, my love?"

"Tomàs. Everything good is from Papa."

"I'm glad I can see that hue and your violet eyes, two colors to ever worship."

"You don't need to see the other colors." She stopped wearing them for him so he wouldn't struggle or get headaches from his blindness to them. "I want you to see me."

His mouth claimed hers, but she dared not shut her lids. To awaken away from this pleasure would surely crush what remained of her soul.

"Ahh humph." A masculine cough followed.

"Barrister Norton, I've found you. The Duke of Cheshire requests a private audience."

Barrington smiled broadly and spun letting the cold air separate them. His joy at gaining the duke's notice was palatable, heart-crumbling.

"Where is he, young man?"

The servant adjusted the collar of his shiny livery. "In the study, sir."

Barrington took a step. Then, as if it dawned upon him that he'd be leaving her, he turned and extended his hand. "This will only take a few minutes."

She took his arm and allowed him to lead her back to her seat.

He kissed her forehead, then disappeared into the crowd.

She should be used to this by now, but every time he left, it felt fresh, cutting a little deeper. Someday he wouldn't return. Then the blade would run clean through.

The servant behind her coughed. He tried muffling the repeated cough by turning his face into his sleeve.

The poor dear thirsted. A dry throat, scorched and sore was almost the worst. Amora lifted a finger, summoning him. When the boy popped near, she pushed her glass of water towards him.

Kneeling, the young servant choked and sputtered. His mouth trembled. "I…I couldn't, ma'am."

Flipping her fan, she covered him from the glare of onlookers, then slid the goblet into the servant's hands. "I insist. It's never good to be in want."

A smile bloomed beneath brightening blue eyes and blonde lashes. He downed the liquid. "Thank you, ma'am. Please don't tell."

Amora nodded. The one thing she'd learned well was keeping secrets.

Barrington plodded behind the servant toward the duke's study. Could his heart hold both joy and sadness? Amora tried to appear supportive, but those eyes of hers said everything, more than he wanted to know. Did she have to think of this as an example of him choosing his work over her again? Did she not know what the duke's support would mean for his career? Imagine London's first mulatto judge.

"This will only take a few moments." He said the words under his breath and tried to make sense of the apprehension she'd cast onto him. Perhaps being with child made her more anxious. Five years of barrenness might do that, too.

"Excuse me, Mr. Norton. Did ye say something?"

Barrington shook his head and returned his focus to Cheshire and the dimly lit corridor. The sound of the music was squelched as if the walls had smothered it within a minute of this trek.

A rush of joy raced up his spine, tightening the knots of expectation in his neck. Battling every day to become the man known for finding and winning with truth had come to fruition. All the questions of his appointment to Lincoln's Inn had been trampled by a perfect court record. Now the Duke of Cheshire, one of the lead reformers in Parliament had need of him.

The servant pointed down a final hall. "The door at the end, sir."

The man bowed and returned to the party, leaving Barrington to take the final leg alone. What did the duke have to discuss and why do so in such privacy, away from all his guests, even his servants?

Getting close to the door, Barrington found it cracked. Voices stirred inside.

"Gaia, I know you are nervous about tonight. Don't be. You are beautiful. The ton will love you, my new duchess."

"William, I should be with Mary. Your daughter said her first words. Mute for so long. You don't know my

12

joy."

"I've prayed for this." His tone sounded of a father's pride, loud and hopeful. "But *our* daughter will have her new mother tomorrow. Tonight at the ball, I need my duchess."

From the small slit between the double doors, the lady, the new Duchess of Cheshire, leaned into the duke. "I will try harder to do this public show for you, if that is what you desire."

The duke chuckled. His tall form enveloped her. "For now. But, later tonight in our chambers, I'll need my wife."

She backed away. Her gauzy gown billowed with each step of retreat. "William, you... I will...be so tired. Mary needs..."

The tall man folded his arms against his waistcoat. "You seem to be avoiding the subject of our chambers. I can be a jealous man, but I didn't think that tendency would be stirred from your devotion to Mary. Gaia, do I not make you happy?"

She pushed back into his arms. "More than anything. Yes. But I...I like just us three. A baby may come. It's so dangerous. My mother died--"

"Gaia, you are a strong woman. When it is time, all will be well." The duke dipped his head to his new bride.

Barrington removed his spectacles and knocked on the door. He didn't like eavesdropping, nor interrupting this moment of privacy, but he needed to tend to his own wife.

The duke came to the door and opened it wide. "Lady Cheshire, I will see you in the main hall. Go mingle with our guests. Find your aunt and sister, but stay out of... I'll be along in a moment."

The lady was pretty with spectacles that glowed. Her face dimpled as she clasped the duke's hand. She was younger than he'd expected and more tan, more so than Amora's creamy cheeks. Neither had the milky-white complexion his fellow barrister's boasted of in their wives. Neither's tone was as indicting as his own.

When she swept by him, Barrington saw the crinkly pattern of her shiny bun, the slight flare to her nose. He knew why the duke wanted to talk privately. His stomach knotted from his deflated ego. Barrington marched inside and waited for the man to confess it.

Cheshire closed the door. "Mr. Norton, I am glad you've come tonight. I've a matter that only you can help with. I'm trying to find records on a relative of my wife's. You've been able to locate all types of documents and secrets."

Barrington looked over his lenses at the man who was almost his height. "I don't typically locate missing items unless it is a part of a crime." He pivoted and moved back to the door. "I can recommend my solicitor, Mr. Beakes."

"It has to be you. No one else will be as sensitive."

Barrington wasn't about games. The truth plain and simple was the best course. He rubbed his chin and turned. "Why would that be? I have a feeling this hasn't anything to do with my trial record."

Cheshire brushed the buttons of his waistcoat. "You are perceptive, and you are known to be a man who can find truth. That is what I need for my wife."

"Then say it plainly. For every moment I'm here, my wife is without me. All who I work for understand I need the complete truth or I cannot help. I despise lies and deception."

The duke squared his shoulders. "My wife is like you. She is a mulatto. I need to find out what happened to the man whose blood she shares. I want shipping records or even a bill of sale uncovered."

Bill of Sale? "The duchess's father was enslaved?"

"She only found out recently that she is of mixed races. Now, I need to give her as much information as possible. But this must be kept discreet. Not everyone is of an open mind. I thought surely you would be."

Barrington knew how narrow his world was. People sized up his race before anything else. That was why he pushed so hard for truth, for perfection. He'd long become the model for that one different friend, or the sole ideal the reformers proclaimed in fighting for the end of slavery or expanding education. Being the only was a heavy load, a gun cocked waiting to misfire.

Tugging on his tailcoat, Barrington hid his growing disappointment. "I'll think on it, your grace and send word."

Cheshire pounded closer. "It will be a great favor to me if you agree to take this upon yourself."

Barrington knew exactly what that meant. It was always better to have powerful allies than enemies. He nodded. "Yes, I will look into it. I cannot promise you anything."

"That's better than nothing. Thank you, Mr. Norton."

Barrington bowed and rotated. He walked down the corridor. It would have been nice to be singled out because of his abilities not his blood.

Yet, with ambition stirring in his veins, he'd use this assignment to prove his capabilities. The duke would see that Barrington was more than just in similar straits as the new Duchess of Cheshire.

When her husband reappeared at the entrance to the party, his face held a long frown; similar to the one he'd brought earlier to Mayfair. Amora's heart clenched. The meeting must not have gone well. What could she say to lift his spirits, to reassure him of his worth despite what the Duke of Cheshire said?

She rose from her seat to go to him. Forget this party. She'd tend to his spirits at home. They should leave now.

When she neared, he plastered his face with a short, tight smile. He surely meant it to keep her from fretting, but that never worked. She and anxiety were soul mates. "Are you ready to leave, dearest?"

His lips puckered as if to answer, but his gaze lifted. His eyes narrowed on someone. "Beakes?"

She turned and winced with frustration. His solicitor, Mr. Beakes headed directly toward them. The man embodied work, more time for Barrington to be somewhere else where he could be injured or worse.

Beakes rent his chocolate greatcoat, putting large gloved hands to his lapels. "Mr. Norton, you have to come with me. Smith. He's asking for you."

A long blast of air left her husband's nostrils. "Smith? I just left him this afternoon. Tell him I will see him in the morning before court."

The man tapped his foot, then shook his head from side to side. "He won't be alive in the morning. Well, not for long. He's going to the gallows tomorrow."

Barrington wrenched the back of his neck. His shoulders slumped. "That wasn't supposed to be for a month."

Beakes shrugged. "Change happens. What do I tell him?"

"Y-e-s. I told him, I'd come if asked. I'll return to Newgate after I drop my beautiful family home." Barrington's voice sounded strained, weighted with obligation. But at which part, Newgate or family? "In an hour or so, I'll visit him."

The solicitor stepped forward pulling at his saggy cravat. He looked very grim with bushy furrowed brows and downturned lips. "He says he wants to tell you that truth. You're not going to risk him changing his mind over a delay?"

What did that mean, and why did Mr. Beakes seem to point his beady eyes at her?

"I'll take Mrs. Norton home, right away for you." The sing-song voice of Cynthia Miller filtered near. The woman clad in a low clinging bodice of bright yellow traipsed near. Her ruby hair reflected the candlelight from the wall sconce. Not a tendril out of place on the vixen.

"How good of you." Barrington clasped Amora's hand. "Please understand. I'll be to Mayfair as soon as I can."

"It's not trouble for me to help, Mr. N-oor-ton." The breathless way Cynthia said his name made the flames in Amora's middle more acute. Would the singer's two-faced tricks to lure Barrington start again?

Forgetting the vixen, Amora reached up and caressed his cheek. She so wanted to be understanding. "Is it that dire?"

Her husband's light eyes had faded even more. He tugged at his lapel and adjusted the brilliant gold pin, his grandfather's gift for acceptance into Lincoln's Inn. "Smith lied to protect someone. If I'd known the truth, I could've helped. An innocent man is going to die in the morning. I have to go to him."

How terrible! Breathless, hurting for him, Amora drew her hand to her mouth.

"If I'd had more time to organize my notes the morning of the trial, I am sure I would've seen the lies. I would've made him admit it. If I'd left..." Barrington's voice became muffled. His Adam's apple shook as he coughed.

The unspoken words stopped her heart. *If he'd left Mayfair on time.* If he hadn't attended his needy wife. This killing would be her fault. When would deaths stop being her fault?

He slid his fingers about her palm and drew the union to his chest. "Please be understanding. If he must die, he should have the opportunity to admit to everything, to go to glory with a clean heart."

No, some secrets should die, never to be said aloud. Amora thought this, felt this everyday with every nightmare. "Will you be very late?"

Mr. Beakes tugged his shoulder. "Time is of the essence. I have to catch up to the runners. There will be another good criminal catch tonight."

Barrington shrugged, then kissed her forehead. "I'll try not to be too late, but this may take a while."

Cynthia gripped Amora's arm. "Run along, Mr. Norton, and don't forget my debut performance week's end. Though you are the busiest barrister, you and Mrs. Norton must attend. It would be like having my brother there." Her tone pitched then lowered like a sorrow-filled harp. "Yes, having Gerald back would be so nice. You must come."

Barrington's lips turned up, then his countenance blanked again. "You're a dear, a credit to your great, late brother, Gerald Miller. Miller was such a good man, but Mrs. Norton can tell you of my work ethic."

On that, Amora could write pages. "No one is as dedicated. Be careful."

"Always." After a kiss to her fingers, he let go of Amora's hand and followed Mr. Beakes.

As she watched her husband, the dedicated barrister, wade through the crowd, sadness whipped through her, spinning her mind like a cyclone. Her palm dropped to her abdomen. Would their family be a priority to him, or another jot on his appointment list?

This son wouldn't be in second place for his doting father. Could she truly be happy if at least something of hers took first place in Barrington's heart?

She blinked away the anxiety building inside her mind, pricking her conscience. He was doing what he felt he must for his career, for their family. With a short breath, she placed a smile to her lips to avoid inciting Cynthia's questions. With this baby, Amora and Barrington would be happy. They just had to be.

Chapter Two: Confession And Omission

The guard fumbled with his heavy keys unlocking the iron door to Smith's cell. Barrington fumed. The gaoler was nowhere to be found, so no answers to why Smith's execution would be rushed. What had changed? And by whose orders?

Finally, the lock clicked. The guard flung the door open, allowing Barrington inside. Smith looked pale, white like the cuffs on Barrington's evening shirt. "You've come, Mr. Norton. I didn't think you would."

Barrington took off his hat and pitched it onto the table. "I am a man of my word. I'm here. Tell me the secrets that has sealed your fate."

The condemned fellow put down the Bible leaves. His fingers shook. "Does hanging hurt much?"

"Not for long. You'll hardly notice when you get the swing of it."

Smith's lips twitched in a half-smile as he nodded.

Trudging to the window, Barrington glanced at the finished platform. Smith's execution would begin at dawn. He fixed his gaze on the cart just outside the window bearing white hoods, the ones that would be draped on the prisoner before affixing the noose. As if a heavy weight sat upon his chest, he inhaled hard forcing air inside his lungs. "You asked for me. I said I would come. I left my wife to be here, so tell me now why you are dying? Maybe I could rouse the Lord Justice to stay this execution."

The rag thin man lifted red rimmed eyes to him. "Barrister, I think it's unfair to die for coining. They should save the noose for true villains like the Dark Walk Abductor."

The man still wanted to talk foolishness. Barrington could be escorting his wife home, enjoying holding her until she slept. Amora had looked so beautiful in her lavender gown, the soft neck frill that fluttered when they danced. It was pure happiness slipping his fingers against the sweet texture of the fine pearls beading her bodice, sculpting the gentle rounding of her abdomen.

She was finally to bear him a child, a son to father. Barrington would be nothing like his own drunken one. No, he'd be a source of pride, not constant ridicule. A sigh sputtered out, releasing a portion of the disappointments filling his lungs.

With a grunt, he stopped his woolgathering and turned his attentions back to Smith. "Coining is an offense against the Crown."

"And abducting and killing women, ain't?"

"All the laws must be obeyed, not just the ones we like. Believe me, if they find the fiend, and the magistrate's runners or the vigilantes don't tear him apart, he will see justice. But I believe it a fantasy like a ghost tale, made up to cover ghastly crimes or wanton runaways."

Smith's eyes widened. The man looked as if he'd

choked on his tongue. "Ain't no fantasy. He's real. The crimes are real."

A tingle set in Barrington's ribs. His internal truth detector niggled. Smith wasn't dying for coining, but something worse. Folding his arms, Barrington decided to indulge him and softened his tone. "That's an old crime. No one's likely to pay almost two years out."

"He's been doing it for at least seven. Maybe more. Not sure if he stopped."

Barrington's ears perked up. His blood heated to full boil. "What are you talking about?"

"I was paid to help him. That's why I die tonight. And if I'd said more, my only brother, he'll die too. My brother is all I have left. That's why I lied. I do deserve death for what I've done, for being in league with the devil. But my brother, he's got a young family. Mouths to feed."

Barrington paced over to Smith and grabbed him up by the shirt collars, shaking the miserable man's bones until they rattled. "What are you saying? You are the Dark Walk Abductor?"

Struggling in Barrington's grasp, the man's head bobbled. "Not me. I don't know his name, but I was in his service."

This was madness.

Ramblings.

Lies.

Evil lies.

"Smith, you have me here to spit falsehoods in my face."

"Not lies. When I die, the proof is gone. I contacted him again a couple of months ago 'cause I needed money. He said he'd help. The next thing I know, the coins he gave me were fakes. They found tools in my flat. He sent a note saying he'd help with the charges."

Barrington tossed the man on the bench. "Where is this note? I suppose it's gone."

Smith nodded. Barrington's innards burned brighter than the sun, hotter than hell's fire. "This fantasy won't save you."

"I've done some bad things, Mr. Norton. All for coins. So it is fitting I should die for coining."

A hundred and five thoughts pressed Barrington's skull but only three could be uttered aloud and maintain his Christianity. "Why tell me now and set me on this fleeting chase? You should've kept it to yourself. Is this a final revenge on me for your conviction?"

"No. But if there's anyone who can figure it out, it's you. You're smart. I don't know who he is, but he has means. I saw him once, tall, gentlemanly looking. I'm about to pay for my years of silence, but you can make him pay for all the bad he's done."

Recognition of his talents from a condemned man wasn't the acclaim he sought. Nor was being saddled with another man's burden. Barrington already bore enough. Wiping at his forehead, he pivoted toward the door. "Goodnight, Mr. Smith. Thank you for wasting my time."

"The abductor took a woman the night of June 10th. No, the 11th, 1813." Almost gagging on his lies, Smith raised his voice higher. "He killed her that night, dumped the body in a ditch. There's got to be a record of her murder. I'm telling you the truth."

A date? That could be checked.

"Find him. Before he gets to my brother, too. He won't be satisfied with just me hanging."

The pleading, the confession warbling Smith's voice could not be ignored. Barrington eased his fingers from the bars and rotated to the prisoner. "How can you be so certain of the date?"

"I was there. I drove the carriage. Check the records. You'll see. A woman's body was found on the next morning on the route from London."

"Where were you headed?"

"South. I don't know where. I know he didn't want to kill her there. He had other plans. He--"

Barrington sliced the damp air with his hand. The motion silenced Smith as if he'd struck his windpipe. The perversion never needed to be mentioned outside of the courts. All had heard the rumors of the shameless treatment of the Dark Walk's victims. Were the horrid tales true?

He rubbed at the back of his neck and addressed the witness, perhaps the only one to these crimes. "So your testimony is that you contacted the Dark Walk Abductor. How did you do it?"

"I left a message with the barkeep near the docks asking for help, a little money to get on my feet. That's how we always contacted each other. He knows I have a brother. My brother and his wife will be targets."

Could Smith be telling the truth? And if he was, did that mean the villain still lived and had the influence to get to Smith, to erect this conviction?

"Mr. Norton, you're married. My brother has a wife, one with a child on the way. I'll die for them tomorrow."

Barrington folded his arms and leaned against the bars, picturing his own wife and child on the way. She probably lit candles in every room she paced awaiting his return. A wave of protection, desire and caution encircled his chest pressing until a tired sigh sneaked out.

"Go after the real villain, Mr. Norton. My brother and his wife are happy, with a baby to come. They are innocent. You're married. Are you happy?"

Happy marriage? Scratching the light scruff of new growth on his jaw, Barrington narrowed his thoughts to his wedding trip and the last three months, the good times in his five-year marriage to Amora. "It's pleasant to find someone whom you can trust, someone who fusses over your eating, someone who ensures the bedchamber is warm enough so your hip doesn't ache." Or who calmed his spirit before a big trial. "You've given me much to think about."

He pivoted again and tapped the bar for the guard.

"Mr. Norton, would you mind waiting a little longer? The pages you left talked about repentance. I'd like to know a little more about that."

In for a pound. If he left now, by the time he made it to Mayfair, Amora would be asleep. *Oh Lord, let her not have one of her nightmares, not without him being there to comfort her.*

Barrington swiped at his brow. Perhaps he could get Smith to admit to more details about the killer for whom he claimed to work. After tomorrow, there wouldn't be another chance to interrogate him.

Amora drummed her fingers against the tufted seat of Miss Miller's carriage. It was dark, stuffy, and reeked of chrysanthemums.

Cynthia had lied to Barrington, saying she'd get Amora straight to Mayfair. Once Barrington left, the tart spent her time, thronged by gentlemen, tipsy in compliments on her singing. Trollop.

Tired and a little nauseous with pressure building below her bosom, she left the woman parked at the threshold of the grand portico. Cynthia stood there, flitting her fan at her audience of men. Maybe she enjoyed waylaying Amora. With all the bucks vying for the vixen, she'd never quit.

Since Barrington worked and Cynthia was being Cynthia, Amora might as well sit back and prepare for her lay-in, the birthing of her child here in chrysanthemum hades.

Another ten or fifteen minutes in the dark sent a wince to Amora's lips. Maybe she could wave at Cynthia to hurry her. Turning to the window, she spied Mr. Charleton. Heart thumping, then bumping to a stop, Amora ducked down, tucking her arms over her head. Did he see her? No no no. He couldn't see her.

She pushed foul air into her lungs, and forced her heart to beat again. A little faster than dead, but not quite a quiet rhythm. If that man knew she was alone, he'd want to converse about the past. Things that should be forgotten. He needed to march away and take the memories too.

Fidgeting, she peeked in time to see the gentleman retreat into the party. Good. No confrontations, no fanning of gossip's flames. No infernos tonight.

The light disappeared as the moon dipped behind the clouds, making everything darker. Could she survive another hour in this small space?

Perhaps she could ask the footman for a lantern. Barrington always read, so riding with him, she never had to beg...beg for light. *Beg.*

A tremor rippled over her body. She gripped her arms about her to try to stop the shivers. Having an episode with Cynthia wouldn't bode well.

Filling her lungs, Amora wiped her brow. After counting twenty-three stars and forty-one nail heads, the carriage door finally opened.

"Sorry to keep you waiting, Mrs. Norton...Amora. My admirers can't get enough."

Cynthia slithered inside, taking the seat opposite her. She tucked her form fitting train against her long legs, and adjusted her red satin cape. "Hope you were comfortable. After all, what is a songstress to do?"

There were a number of things, Amora could list: stay away from Barrington, stop using her dead brother's memory to twist her husband into knots. Those pronouncements wouldn't be received well, so she made her tone pleasant. "I'm happy for you. You're the rage of London."

The carriage rocked and swayed forward. Hopefully, they'd take the short path back to Mayfair, about twenty minutes of finger counting. With the longer way, it would be difficult to think of more compliments for this *friend* of Barrington's.

"I have done well with the cards I've been dealt. But I'd give it all away for the love of a good man like...oh, I don't know. Someone like Mr. Norton."

One, two, three. She tried to ignore the viper's venom, but it stung her chest to imagine Cynthia with Barrington. Amora smoothed her pinkie over the stitches of her shawl's hem. She must remain even-tempered, bland like the simple cloth shrouding her shoulders. "The weather is nice. Not too hot or cold."

"Is that all you have to say? We're alone. You could show off your wit. Well, you used to be witty."

No doubt, if Amora lost her temper, Cynthia would

tell Barrington, ending the newly found peace of the Norton marriage. Nothing was worth that.

"Well, I can be civil too. The weather is delightful. See we can convey to Mr. Norton our nice conversation. That should please him. Don't you want to please him?"

This woman must possess something that made Barrington blind to Cynthia's faults. But what?

Truthfully, Amora would love for Barrington to miss her flaws, just like he missed the colors red and green.

Tired of careful speech, she grimaced. "You want something, Miss Miller, other than my husband. Or you would be following him to the prison, offering to hold his hand as he walked the corridors."

Cynthia laughed. "You are a sly one. I need Barrington to represent someone dear to me, but I know he won't if he thinks it will upset you."

"My husband attends clients, with or without my approval." Amora bit her lip. She couldn't alert the singer to any marital difficulties.

"You can brag a little. You have more power over him than you think. No, it's going to take your urging to get Barrington to agree."

"Why would I help? You make veiled threats at taking my husband. Do you think I'm a fool?"

Cynthia slipped closer, planting her painted face directly in front of her. "I'm not the only one who'd love to borrow him, even for just a little while. His father was quite the man about town, and most men of Barrington's stature have mistresses. Usually a trinket or two keeps the wives happy."

A trinket? Or a bauble, like a pearl necklace. An ache stabbed her middle. She bit back the pain. The jade couldn't know her words cut deep.

With a lift of her chin, Amora leveled her shoulders. She hid her balled fists in the folds of her shawl. "Mr. Norton is not most men. He's quite honorable."

"He is a dear, but all males have limits. They can be driven into willing arms." She snatched a fan out of her reticule and whipped it about in the stale air. "Very willing arms."

There was no doubt, no misunderstanding of her words. Cynthia intended to seduce Barrington.

"Yet, I could consider leaving him alone."

Amora cut her gaze to the treacherous jade. "What?"

"I need you to let him take my case. It's life or death for my family. I wouldn't be here trying to seek this favor, humbling myself before you, if it weren't grim."

"If it's such, Mr. Norton will make the right decision."

"Not if working so closely with me, day and night, will upset you. Don't play the helpless wife. You are a force to be reckoned with, though Barrington says you don't paint any more or play the pianoforte. Afraid my talents will outshine yours, so you abandon the competition?"

Cynthia and Barrington discussed her? A lump formed in her throat. She forced herself to swallow.

"Will you support me?" The tart leaned forward. An errant curl flopped from her carefully coiffed bun.

A glimpse of streetlight exposed her narrowing emerald eyes and thinned lips. "You must agree."

"I can't tell him what to do."

"What if I promise never to tell of your little indiscretion?"

Amora pivoted to the window. She didn't want to think of that time, but the memories returned almost every night. More so, when Barrington wasn't home. A shudder rippled through her. Would she ever be free of them?

Cynthia gripped Amora's arm. "Look at me."

The woman's silhouette seemed similar to her lost cell mate's, but that girl was kind. No cruelness in her, that precious soul.

"I know you didn't tell him of your *disappearance*? So, he married a liar." Cynthia giggled. The notes weren't merry, but harsh and threatening. She tightened her hold.

The pressure hurt as did the pain in Amora's abdomen. She snatched her hand free. "Stop this now. You wouldn't want Mr. Norton to know of this unsightly nature."

Cynthia eased back onto her seat. Her fingers flicked at the bunches of fabric crowding her feet. "Barrington knows everything, everything about me. He was so caring about my child out of wedlock. If I'd been able to keep her, he'd treat the lass as if she were his."

Amora closed her eyes. Was that a hint? No, Barrington would have told her, if he and the singer... Her mind wouldn't complete the sentence. "Mr. Norton loves children. He'll never condemn a child for the mother's failings."

A hiss filled the dim cabin. "When he learns of your failing, we'll see if you're still so smug. We know how he hates liars, and you wed without disclosure. No man wants to be married in darkness."

The blood in Amora's veins froze. She chiseled free her gaze and peered through the glass. She spied the sign, Conduit Street. That was one block from the townhouse. She tapped on the roof of the carriage. With the gas street lamps burning, she could run and be on their Mayfair doorsteps within minutes. "Out! I want out!"

Her shriek did the trick. The carriage stopped. A footman appeared and opened the door. Amora stood and extended her hand to be let down.

"Oh, no, Mrs. Norton. I told Barrington I'd take you home. I'm not going to be accused of dropping you anywhere but your house."

"I'll take my chances. Besides, he'll forgive you." Amora leapt out of the carriage and wrapped her shawl tight about her trembling limbs.

"Suit yourself." The door slammed shut and the carriage moved away at a fast clip.

Even if she wanted to change her mind, it was too late. The carriage and horses disappeared at the end of the street. Amora filled her lungs with the chilly air. Staring at the lit street lamps, she paced toward the townhome.

The shuffle of her satin slippers echoed. The darkness of the night crowded her, squeezing her lungs, bringing heavy breath after breath pouring out of her mouth.

Shaking, she gripped her tummy. "One, two, three." Counting aloud usually slowed her thoughts, but not tonight. Images of a darkened cellar with roots pushing through the floor crowded her head. The noise of falling brick clogged her ears. A sour taste rose from her stomach, drying her tongue.

If she blinked, she could be lost again, waiting in the dank prison, listening for the horrid footsteps of her abductor.

The shadows of trees swept across her path.

Her heart slammed against her chest.

Something was coming for her.

Even in London, she couldn't hide.

By the time she stumbled onto Mayfair's first step, the stabbing ache in her abdomen cut through her every few seconds. She couldn't stop shivering.

Pounding on the door, she sank to her knees.

It opened. Mrs. Gretling stood in the threshold bundled in a thick woolen robe holding a candle. "Mrs. Norton, are you alright?"

She fell against her housekeeper. The world grew darker, wrapping Amora in pure blackness.

With each weighted step, Barrington dragged into his carriage. His heart hung heavy, filled with hopeless burdens. The execution had lasted ten minutes. Ten whole minutes.

One to line up the men on the platform. A couple more to slip white hoods over Smith and the others. Another two to hear the building cheers of the wretched crowd. Then less than thirty seconds to feel the reverberation of the drop of the platform. Thud, Thud.

Ten minutes, the difference between life and death.

Barrington stretched out on the seat. The clip-clop of his horse team couldn't distract him from Smith's confession. Or the knowledge Barrington had been used to bring about Smith's death.

The fellow was innocent of coining, but not of this Dark Walk Abductor business? The clear-eyed confession. The palm-sweat Smith kept wiping on his breeches as he recounted of his vile participation in acquiring victims. A man facing death wouldn't lie about such evil transactions, would he?

Yet, one lie begat another. What words could be trusted from a liar's tongue.

Barrington rubbed at his skull. He had a date and a

crime to give to his solicitor. Beakes was good at finding details. He'd put him on it later today once he made amends to Amora. How mad could she be?

The carriage stopped outside the jewelers. At well past ten in the morning, Bond Street typically hosted crowds of shoppers. Barrington didn't have the energy to face any of it and remained upon his seat with his eyes closed.

Hopefully, his man-of-all-work was the first in line at the merchant. The silversmith should be finished with the rattle. A husband needed something to smooth any new thorns that might await him at home. One lesson he'd learned from watching his father drag in at all hours. A good distraction offered a chance at peace.

The dainty bauble, no bigger than his thumb, etched with his and Amora's initials should distract her. She'd think of their child and forget how late he was.

Maybe she'd realized that even if he weren't with her, she was very present in his thoughts. *Oh, Lord, let her understand.* A few months of happiness weren't enough.

The door to the carriage opened. A refreshing breeze blew inside. "Sir."

Barrington stretched and blinked at James.

His man, dressed in a dark coat steeped in braided trim, poked his ruddy face inside. "Here, sir."

"Thank you." Barrington took the velvet pouch. The smooth nape appeared gray, but it was probably emerald or red. How horrid not to experience all the shades of a rainbow. On the balcony, Amora had said she wanted him to see her. Clothing was one thing, but she shouldn't have given up painting, something that had once brought her joy. He'd speak to her about that.

Yet, his inability to detect certain hues didn't explain why she'd also abandoned the pianoforte. He adored music, and she was quite proficient before the war.

"Mr. Norton, I took a peek inside. Just lovely."

James's infectious grin filled his countenance. If not for the solemn night or the possibility of facing an angered wife, Barrington would smile too.

"The missus should love it. Might do the trick. You won't have to lounge in your study."

"Hope so. Get me home as quickly as possible."

"Yes, but be at ease. One night isn't long enough to change the locks." His man shut the door and soon the carriage raced towards Mayfair.

James was of a different race, different station in life, but no one understood Barrington's burdens better. Hopefully, his man was right about the locks, too.

Running a hand against his hair, Barrington shoved on his top hat and tried to relax. Nothing could ease his soul. Since the onset of her pregnancy, he'd been very careful to be in by at least ten each evening.

This should be a happy time for them both. His being absorbed in work always made her uneasy. Headaches, nightmares. He'd find her upset in her chambers, stewing as if she assumed something bad had happened.

With a last tweak to his wilted cravat, he bounded from the carriage.

"Good luck, sir." James tipped his tricorn hat and tugged the reins of the conveyance, hauling beasts and carriage toward the mews.

Partially blinded by the glare of the bright sunlight, Barrington plodded up the path and onto the portico. All the lights of the house were a glow. Amora had a penchant for burning candles, but this was a bit much. Why?

He pressed on the door. It opened before he could

settle his fob in the keyhole. Not locked?

Mrs. Gretling pounded down the steps with a bucket of balled up sheets. "Oh, Mr. Norton! You're home. No one knew where to find you."

Her tone sounded clipped. Their Scottish housekeeper was not shy with her opinions, but Amora knew where he was.

"My wife didn't say?"

The housekeeper shook her head. Her face pinched as she ran towards the kitchen. Were those tears in her light eyes?

Amora. He turned toward the stairs, but two men blocked his way. He recognized one as the physician who looked after Amora's odd headaches about eight months ago. But who was the other, the lanky man with walnut colored hair parted and converging upon a low brow?

And why were they coming from Amora's bedchamber?

The physician stopped in front of him and extended his hand. His countenance was ashen. "Mr. Norton…"

The other man also stuck his hand in Barrington's face. "I am Reverend Samuel Wilson. I wish we met under different circumstances."

Eyes widening until they hurt, a feeling of utter dread ripped Barrington's gut asunder. He pushed through them and pounded up the stairs to Amora's chamber.

Chapter Three: The Pain and Promise of Choices

Barrington flung open the door and stopped at the foot of her bed. How grey her skin looked. How small and hopeless her ragged breathing sounded. She seemed lost, maybe gone from him. *Please be alright.*

He made his wooden legs move forward. He rounded the side of her canopy bed and eased onto the mattress. A bandage wrapped her forearm, poking out beneath her muslin robe. Spots darkened the wrapping. Had the doctor blood let her? "Amora?"

Afraid to touch her. Afraid not to, he stroked her shoulder. "Can you hear me?"

Her lids opened. One shaky hand lifted then fell against his waistcoat. Her fingertips struck the buttons, jingling them. "Barr?"

"Oh, sweetheart. You? The baby?"

With a wince, she pushed away and rolled deeper into the bedclothes. "No. N-o-o baby, no baby."

The quaking in her voice, the finality of her words

gripped his heart, squeezing it until nothing but sorrow wrung out. He couldn't breathe, couldn't put a name to any thought, couldn't imagine how all their hopes were gone.

"My fault. M-y fault."

Her cold whisper echoed rattling against the now-empty cavity within his chest. "No, sweetheart, not at all. You're alive."

He hadn't lost everything. They hadn't lost everything. "Things will be well. We will be fine. Oh, and I love you."

She slipped away a little more. The distance could be a mile. A mile in the bed where he'd held her, listened to her raspy giggle against his chest, where they locked fingers, lips, and soul ties, where they'd made this child.

Where they'd made this child lost.

Where he'd held her every night, except this last.

"Go work, Barr."

He stirred up his most convincing voice, the one he'd use for Justice Burns when a witness lied and he had to appeal for mercy. "If I'd known, I would've been here. You know that. I should've been here. This is my fault."

"Hope gone."

The pain in her voice, cut a little more of him, dumped his work-ethic beliefs into the rubbish bin. If only he'd been here. If only.

Throat closing, he sucked in air. Barrington brushed her temples, wrapping a lock of fever-damp hair about his thumb. "I'm here now. Tell me how to make things better."

Her shuttered breath told the truth. There was no better.

Slipping betwixt the covers, he crawled next to her,

just as he should have done last night and towed her into his embrace. Her body felt stiff, none of her typical softness, no loving limbs curling into his chest. She must wish him gone, but how could he leave?

Her clammy palm gripped his and pulled it to her abdomen. "Only thi... holdi... your ...tention died."

Her womb felt so empty and flat beneath his fingertips. She'd just started to show.

How could he hold in the violent storm brewing in his conscience? He dug inside and found some strength, something made from his grandfather's will. He couldn't appear broken in front of her. She needed him strong. He needed to be strong. "I'm so sorry, my love."

She turned toward him. Her hands caught on his jacket. The pouch fell from his pocket. The silver rattle jingled onto the mattress.

Her thumbs slipped over it before jabbing it into his gut. "No bauble. Leave." She sighed and then began to sob. "Leave."

His spectacles steamed. He popped the useless gift into his pocket and dragged himself from the room.

With a closed door as the final separation between them, he sank against the wall in the hall. He wasn't built of stone, nor enslaved to his emotions, but this had no logic, no reasoning. Just pain.

He was empty, empty with a hole just as big and as deep as when his best friend, Gerald Miller died. A friend so much closer than his own brother. Miller had died in Barrington's stead.

Why God? If he'd let Smith perish alone, not knowing redemption... Would that have been better?

If he'd only chosen to take Amora home. Maybe it would've made a difference. At least, he could've been with her and not let her face this agony with strangers.

He ripped off his spectacles, closing them within his palms so tight it felt as if they'd break. This one time in three months, he chose something over her. That equaled the death of his child? Amora hating him?

He swallowed the hard lump in his throat. It didn't go away.

His Blackamoor love wasn't enough-- the heart of a dull, color-robbed man wasn't enough. He'd just proved it, by not being here to protect her or their child. "God, I was away doing your work, not out carousing or imbibing. Why couldn't you have been here with my wife, my child?"

The pounding on the stairs drew Barrington's weary attention to the man he'd seen earlier.

"God was here, Mr. Norton. But some things aren't meant to be."

Barrington scooped up his lenses, thrust them on and turned to the intruder, the wild haired vicar from the entry. Wilson's outstretched hand hovered inches away.

This time Barrington took it. He allowed the older man, maybe six or seven years his senior, to hoist him upright.

"Mr. Norton, I am about His business and sometimes the path is sorrowful. Even Job cried, and none of us could carry his heavy burdens."

Barrington pushed past him. He wasn't going to open his soul to a stranger. "Follow me."

With listless steps, he led the man down the stairs to his prized room. Once inside, he closed the door. "Sit, Vicar. I'd offer you something to drink, but I don't have anything strong. Though my late father could conjure something drunken from the kitchen." He bit his lip.

This wasn't James he complained to but a minister, a stranger at that. "Did the doctor or Mrs. Gretling summon you?"

"I was playing cards with the doctor when the footman arrived. The message was so dire; I came along to see if I could bring comfort. I'm helping at St. George's for a season. My living in Hampshire will be vacated soon."

Barrington paced from his perch against a bookshelf. He walked past the vicar and dropped into the chair behind his desk. Once he pushed stacks of paper out of the way, he viewed the vicar with open suspicion. "You're from Hampshire? We're from there. Clanville to be exact."

"I know of the Nortons and your wife's Tomàs family. As a boy, I used to visit my cousin, Minister Playfair, in your village."

The man knew of them? Barrington drummed his fingers along the desk, trying hard to order his thoughts given the stranger's advantage of foreknowledge. "Oh, the old vicar."

"Yes. Playfair was a wonderful mentor. I loved fishing with him at the stream behind the smithy, close to the priory. Lots of good tackle. Tasty trout."

Cheery, almost skipping, the vicar's tone reflected boyish hope. To Barrington it grated, reminding him of another place he'd never show his son. Another memory to be shed from his list.

Wilson puffed up his chest, sitting back with folded arms. "Clanville. I loved playing in the creepy priory, the old Norman temple. And I had been known to steal a few of Mr. Tomàs's pippins. That sweet juicy apple was almost worth the lecture. A powerful, lighthearted man,

Mr. Tomàs."

"My father-in-law, Mr. Tomàs, was a good man." Barrington held his tone steady, tried to keep it and his thoughts rooted there, not Tomàs's worse half, his mother-in-law. While his father-in-law was a firebrand - warm and encouraging, the shrew was a blizzard - cold and mean.

The weight of the morn fell again upon his shoulders, forcing him to slouch. He rested his aching hip against the well-worn chair. The bullet wound, Napoleon's parting present from the war. "Was my wife in much pain?"

The man's bushy brow lifted. He raked through his tousled hair. What words did he search for? How much more horrible could the events be?

"She was quite fevered. She said…she said some odd things."

The undercurrent in his voice held accusations. How did Barrington not think more of Amora's needs? How sorry was the state of their marriage? How would they get on after this loss? Accusations Barrington couldn't answer.

"Has your wife ever been institutionalized?"

Barrington sat up. Every muscle in his face tensed, almost snapping. "No. I don't know what you've come to peddle, but she is not in any state that needs to be sent away."

"I was not suggesting anything of the sort. It was her fear of the doctor, her begging not to be locked away. She seemed to be reliving something."

Barrington glanced at Wilson's jaw, the place he'd strike first if he let his temper free. "Just a nightmare. A delusion from the pain of losing our child."

"My late wife, she miscarried a few years before birthing my boy. She took a tumble in the garden. She was never that healthy again." He cleared his throat and lifted his gaze. "Mrs. Norton had a lot of pain, almost too much pain."

Barrington's heart broke again. Unlike the vicar, Amora still lived. "Sorry about your wife, Wilson."

"I've reconciled with it, Mr. Norton. God gave us ten beautiful years. He gives and He takes away." He leaned forward. "The next few months won't be easy ones for Mrs. Norton. My wife was plagued with guilt. Me too, for not being there to catch her. Taking in a foundling child was a saving grace."

"I see." Barrington looked down at his mahogany desk, inherited from his grandfather. With his thumb, he traced the etches, and then scooted papers along the blotter atop. Maybe they'd never have children. Would that be fine, no son with his skin, her eyes?

"With your permission, I'd like to visit with Mrs. Norton in a few days."

Something in his tone didn't sound like a ministerial visit. No, it seemed dire.

Barrington raised his head, glaring at the vicar. "What do you suspect?"

Wilson stood and pressed his hands along the edge of the desk, between the piles of correspondence. "I've seen signs similar to hers, and these women became so desperate they took their lives. I won't let that happen again."

Gut burning, Barrington jumped up and stepped into the minister's shadow. "My wife has never possessed such weakness. I will help her. She will be fine. Get out, vicar. Never come back."

The fellow nodded and left the room.

Barrington heard the front door close. He sank into his chair and drew the rattle out of his pocket. He shook it, listening to the tinkles that sounded like flapping angel wings. He wondered how different things would be if he or God had chosen to be at Mayfair with Amora.

Chapter Four: Something's Keeping You From Me

Amora sat at her vanity pulling curl papers from her hair. Four weeks of doing nothing but eating warm porridge and milk may have strengthened her limbs but did nothing for her restless mind.

Since that horrid night, Barrington sat with her every day, bringing her the milk, reading her Shakespeare and bits of case law.

Not once did he mention the miscarriage. Not once did he accuse or condemn her.

He should yell or prepare his summation assigning guilt.

She lost their child. How much worse could his charges be than the ones repeating in her head?

Pretending nothing was wrong was her suit, not his. Offering her kindness and sad looks couldn't change anything. Her eyes stung but they were long dried of tears. Keeping the babe safe in her bosom was her only job and she failed. Why did she let horrid Cynthia work her into a frenzy? Why did Amora believe she could walk a block in the dark without her nightmares chasing her?

She dropped her head into her hands and pushed at her sorry temples, trying to force the memories from her brain. But they were with her. Always would be.

Maybe she should just tell Barrington of her *disappearance* as Cynthia put it.

If she'd blurted it out after all these years, what would Barrington say?

Could he understand the terror of being dragged from Papa's orchard? No, he'd think her foolish for painting so far from Tomàs Manor, away from her mother's watchful eye.

And if he'd known, the shame would've forced him to abandon Amora, never marrying her. Maybe it would have been best if they never wed. It had to be better than continually disappointing him.

Than losing his child.

Her heart hung low. Those dry eyes sprung a new droplet. The truth would send him to "willing arms". Marriage wouldn't prevent it. A difficult wife, one with lies, would give him ample excuse.

She rubbed her sleeves. Her skin suddenly chilled thinking of Cynthia in Barrington's arms, bearing him a babe. No. The cold truth had to remain a secret.

A knock echoed from outside her bedchamber.

Her breath caught. Barrington? She straightened and tugged the remaining papers from her tresses. "Come in."

The door opened. It was only Mrs. Gretling.

Relief and disappointment battled within Amora's lungs. Relief won.

Tartan skirts flapping, her housekeeper brought a basket of linens and snowy chemises to the closet and began moving one muted frock and then another. "Mrs. Norton, it's so good to see ye up."

"I thought it about time to move about. Next, I'll try being useful." She bit her lip. No need to affirm her sad state.

Mrs. Gretling traipsed closer and offered one of her I-pity-you looks with her scrunched up sherry eyes. "It's Thursday. Would you like to go with me to the hospital?"

"What?" Her pulse pounded as visions of a high table and tight leather straps crossed her mind's eye. She lowered her shaking hands to her lap. "I don't..."

One silvery eyebrow rose higher on her abigail's long face. "I meant the Foundling Hospital, ma'am. You usually go with me."

Oh, the abandoned children, the poor orphans. Amora blinked a few times and waited for her pulse to return to normal, whatever normal was. "I can't see a precious babe someone gave away." She shook her head. "I'm not ready."

"Maybe next week." She set down the basket and wiped her hands on her thick apron before fluffing Amora's spiraling locks. "Hurry, you can have breakfast with the master."

Stunned, she clasped Mrs. Gretling's hands to stop her primping. "Mr. Norton's not at court?"

"No, he's been having his breakfast here most days.

Fishing a ribbon through Amora's tresses, she pinned up the chignon. "I think he liked the pattern you two set before. Oh, listen to me run on. Go see him."

Mrs. Gretling took up her empty basket, then shuffled back through the doorway. "He's devoted to you, you know."

The door closed, leaving Amora even more confused.

Barrington kept at their routine, even with no baby?

No, there had to be another reason. Maybe she should find out. After smoothing her dark gray, almost black muslin bodice, she took step after step until she crept to the other side of her door.

With a glance, she gaped at the stairs leading below to the first floor and then the one to the upper levels and attic.

What would he say when he saw her out of her bedchamber? Would he measure his words and offer a dutiful kiss on the forehead, one meant for his poor sick wife? What if he were just waiting for her to be strong enough to tell her he didn't, couldn't love her anymore?

The day he discovered she carried his child, he canceled all his appointments and had James take them for a long carriage ride. Barrington chased away her nausea by feeding her sweet ice from Gunter's. He'd kissed her between spoonfuls of the lemony goodness.

No, nothing compared to when he was truly happy with her. Pity, those moments were rare.

She clamped her fingers onto the rail then paced up the treads. She'd rather go to the attic and imagine she'd climbed Papa's oak. There she could pretend her mind was well, her marriage whole.

The door to the large space creaked open and exposed a room filled with portmanteaus and old furnishings. Dust filled the air, but no other place in the house had better windows. The leaded panes let in London's sun. When it showered, a rainbow became visible and the glass cast orange and blue hues on the walls. Color.

She stepped deeper inside and saw her crimson trunk. With a little bit of grunting, she tugged it closer to the window. Her wardrobe before their marriage was stashed in the big leather box.

Barrington had the top mantua-maker on Bond Street design her matronly gowns in "becoming" colors, heavily textured fabrics for his fingers. He gave Amora little say, calling them presents. If she'd spoken up and expressed her displeasure, he may have listened. Maybe. Maybe not.

Well, since she wasn't going to get any bigger any time soon, she wouldn't need to purchase new silks of gold or woolens of sage.

A moan slipped from her throat. Loss swept in again and filled her vacant insides. No baby.

Why did his god hate her so much?

Hadn't she suffered enough?

She eased onto the windowsill and coddled her empty middle, rubbing her palms repeatedly over the sad muslin fabric.

A diversion. That's what she needed. No more thinking about what couldn't be changed. Opening the trunk, she sunk her hands into an emerald gown and a garnet shawl. She remembered music, dancing with Papa wrapped in these treasures. Colors. She missed seeing them. Painting was once like breathing.

Her knuckles ached a little. She looked down. Her fingers had clenched as if she played Papa's pianoforte.

A duet of Haydn's music with her father always made her smile. One-two-three, one-two-three. Oh, she missed his music most of all. Papa would stick in an extra chord in the refrain, something that only she would catch. Their private joke. Others thought it original to the tune. Thinking of him, she felt lighter, found herself humming.

Digging deeper, she found a walking dress of dark

blue, a bonnet with bright puce ribbon. Nothing pale or dull in this box. Mother bought many gowns to make amends for not believing Amora and for every unkindness she'd rendered.

Liar.

Harlot.

Sorry.

Forgive me.

Forgiving her mother was a hopeless gesture for Amora. A sigh blasted out. What was left if you couldn't remember the past without anger, and now you hated the present?

She took her fisted hand and punched deeper into the box, down to her old painting smock. The red and bronze stains. She hadn't had a chance to sponge them. An argument with her grieving mother had sent Amora running to the orchard with just paint, a canvas, and an easel. That afternoon, the sun warmed the thick heather grasses as her garnet skirts danced at her feet. Then a hit from behind and blackness.

Her nightmares tried to restore her missing memories of what happened next. Maybe she should just give in and remember the monster in the dark. Shaking, she fisted her hands. "Nothing to do with you."

She covered her mouth and thought of the one person who always believed in her. Papa. His love was constant. He'd have chased her nightmares away, and wouldn't think her weak or changed because of it.

He would've rescued her.

Swallowing, she peered again into the trunk. Her fingers landed on an old leather case. A faint scent of tart turpentine pushed out. Her old paint set. Mother must've stuck it in here.

Were the brushes inside?

For the first time in years, the urge to create gripped her spirit. Her thumb and palm burned where a pallet should be.

Barrington ran into the room. "There you are!"

Heart slammed against her ribs as if she'd been caught doing something naughty. She lifted from the box and dropped the lid.

"I didn't mean to frighten you. I just wanted..." He sucked in a deep breath as if he'd been chasing a villain. His face glowed brick red, almost fevered.

Was he sick? "Barrington, has something happened?"

He cleared his throat and came closer. "I just had to see you."

Marching past her, he headed straight to the window. His palms went over the glazing and the old latch. "It hasn't opened in years."

A swish of air released from his nostrils as he ran a hand over his lapel.

"Are you well, Barrington? You seem disturbed."

He pivoted, stepped back to her and pulled her into his arms.

She went stiffly. Her body wedged against him, as warm as a wooden plank.

"Something the vicar said made me very concerned, but it's nonsense. You'd come to me if you were troubled. No matter how angry you are, you know you can confide in me."

His arms held her tight against his charcoal waistcoat. "I know you feel sometimes as if I don't love you enough. Yes, things are different. But we haven't drifted so far apart."

She pushed at his shoulders, but he wouldn't let her

go. Instead he stroked her back, caressed her curves with his big hands.

They'd shared a bed almost every night. Of course he knew how to make her melt into him. Did he still want her, even with no baby?

"You can tell me anything, Amora. There's nothing, we can't face together."

"Anyth--"

His mouth was on hers before she could say more. Fingers on her waist tickled, cajoled. Others rummaged her curls, easing the strain in her neck.

If the truth came out, would he desire her then? No, he wouldn't. She gave his waist a shove. "No. Barrington."

"Please, Amora. Just take my love. I'll make it enough. This time I will."

His deep voice sounded as if he'd finished a court argument. He lifted her chin and took her mouth again. Yet, his reasoning was merely passion. Would it be sufficient?

She could make her arms willing, until she figured things out. It wasn't hard when Barrington was sweet and kissed her as if he needed to sample the air trapped in her lungs.

She clasped her palms on his lapels ruining his perfect cravat. Clinging to him, she hoped to feel his heart. This could be one of the last times she'd know its heavy beat. He'd want nothing to do with her when Cynthia made good on her threat.

Barrington kissed her more deeply. His heart felt ragged and bruised. When Mrs. Gretling said Amora had gone to the attic, all he could think about was the vicar's stupid warning. An image of her jumping headlong from the high window filled him.

Daft vicar. At least the thought of losing Amora shook Barrington from his fog. He flew up the stairs, as if he had wings.

God might be busy again, so it must be Barrington's responsibility alone to protect his wife. He'd ignored earlier signs of her distress and thought her unease was simply hesitation to attend the party. God gave warnings, but it was up to Barrington to act upon them.

Oh, she was so soft, so perfectly curved. Even with all her flaws, no one made him this crazed, made this man of logic lose all reason. He scooped her from the floor, higher into his arms. The buttons on the sleeves of her dark gown bore into his muscles. He didn't care. He couldn't get enough of her warm lips shivering beneath his.

If only they could come to an understanding. Maybe if he never stopped kissing her, all would be well.

He'd do better at making her happy. He owed it to her for not being with her when she miscarried, for leaving her to grieve with strangers.

His thumbs caught in the back seam of her gown. A desire to shelter her, to prove his new commitment, made him tug at the muslin.

"Barrington." She pushed at his shoulders. "I'm not ready."

Oh, that lack of reason. He very well couldn't love her so soon after a miscarriage or take her on the hard floor of the dusty attic. He relented and lowered her until her slippers again touched the ground. "We lost the baby and that broke our hearts, but we must go on. There could be another child, one with your violet eyes. We haven't lost us."

She pulled up her sleeve. "Things weren't well before I was pregnant. What if I'm not meant to carry a babe? I may never be blessed with that joy." She rubbed her temples. "I can't stand to see a doctor covering up another poor--"

He put a finger to her lips. His innards shredded at the agony in her voice. She shouldn't relive their baby's loss. "Don't give up on us."

"Mr. Norton, it's time to go. You'll be late for court." James's merry voice fell upon Barrington's shoulder. Horrid timing.

"I'll be down soon. Pull the carriage around." He closed his eyes as the weight of his trial load fell into remembrance.

Amora stepped away from him. "You should go. Don't be late."

"I've been remiss these past weeks missing a number of sessions, but my mentor and colleagues understand. They wish you well."

Her cheeks darkened as she repinned her gown. "Oh, I see."

"I even missed Miss Miller's debut. Gerald up in heaven will just have to understand, there's only one woman I'm concerned about."

"Concerned?" She spun toward the window. "I'm feeling better. You can go to the Old Bailey or visit with Gerald's sister."

Why did it feel as if he'd thrown icy water on Amora? She even rubbed her arms as if she were chilled. "Yes, Cynthia is alone. I promised Gerald as he took his last breath to watch over her."

"Keep your promises. Go to work." She pivoted and

waved at him as if he were a stray pup. "Miss Miller or a client needs you more."

Why did she feel threatened by his responsibilities? His work was important. His clients needed him too. Beakes might've learned more about the date Smith offered on the eve of his execution. The frustration swelling in his heart threatened to explode. "Amora, you're not being fair."

"Life is not fair. Leave me. I want you to go."

The temptation to pull her back into his arms hurt, twisting his gut. Maybe he could shirk his responsibilities one more day. Would that prove his devotion?

She took another step away. Her countenance held no smile, just narrowing violet eyes. "Have a good day."

Gut roiling, he pivoted. Arguing at the Old Bailey would release the tension caught in his limbs. When would he get this marriage balance right?

He dragged to the steps. "I'll be home early for dinner."

Her face remained blank, even as she nodded.

A chill swept through him as she moved to the window seat. What if she didn't want him to get it right? What if this loss gutted her longing for their marriage, her longing for him?

No, he'd prove himself to her. He'd not disappoint her again.

Chapter Five: Truth Should Set You Free

Thank goodness for Thursday. Thursday meant newborns at the Foundling Hospital and that was a reason for Amora to pretend that she was better. Barrington and Mrs. Gretling wouldn't let her come if they suspected how low her spirits sat. Cynthia hadn't gotten Barrington's attention yet, but she would.

How miserable it was to wait each day for Barrington to come home filled with accusation or worse to not come home, too shamed and disgusted.

Liar.

Harlot.

Sorry.

Forgive me.

She rubbed her temples to force away the sounds of her mother's and Barrington's voices blending in evil pronouncements.

"Mrs. Norton?"

Amora blinked a few times and adjusted the babe in her arms. "Yes."

The duchess of Cheshire looked over the smallish crib

in the corner. "Mrs. Norton, I am so glad you've chosen this to be your charity."

Nodding at the friendly smile, Amora rocked the orphaned boy, tucking a blanket under his chubby chin. "Yes, I can think of no greater cause than to help the defenseless."

The young woman smiled genuinely. Her lips curled up into something true and honest.

She wasn't what Amora thought of as a duchess. Not stuffy or pretentious, the duchess didn't put on airs. She used her hands for the care of children and that took a special heart. When the duchess mentioned her husband, she glowed like a new bride should.

Amora closed her eyes for a moment remembering when Barrington finally came for her. For a month maybe, she looked like Lady Cheshire with stars in her eyes, but stars only shine at night. And night brought bad memories. Then terror came anew.

Now it started to creep into her day, waking dreams.

"Mrs. Norton. Mrs. Norton? Are you well?"

Shivering, Amora looked up. "Yes." She waited for her rising pulse to settle and counted the babe's sniffle snores. It took over thirty for the chill in her arms to go away and for her brain to accept that she was safe in the Foundling Hospital, years and miles away from the monster.

The duchess smoothed her Sardinian blue bodice and headed for the door. "Well, I am going to start story time with the older girls. I hope to see you next week. I don't know very many people in London. I'd like to start with furthering our acquaintance. The duke thinks highly of Mr. Norton."

Amora nodded. "Yes, Duchess."

The woman began to move but stopped. "I'm perfectly serious, Mrs. Norton. I'd like to get to know you better."

With a final beaming smile, the duchess left.

A friend in London. A friend anywhere would be nice. The last time she had a friend…

What was the girl's name? Sky-blue eyes. Gold Hair. Why couldn't she remember?

Mrs. Gretling soon sailed inside wearing her satisfied smile. Things must be going well with all of her errands around the hospital.

She came close and peaked at the blanket. "How are ye doing with this tiny man, Mrs. Norton?"

"He's settled. His little lips are puckering from a little wind in his belly that tugged his gums."

"He looks very happy with ye, ma'am. But it's time to put the babe down." Mrs. Gretling's sherry eyes flickered from the door to the line of cribs. "You've had him up for awhile and we can't take him with us."

Did her abigail think Amora would run out of the hospital with the child in tow? Yes, she wanted a child, but abducting anyone was beyond the pale. "Not done showing… umm, Tomàs, the room." The babe looked like Papa, with fat cheeks and a bald head. "This one was left on the steps of St. Georges. Only a dented thimble to mark him."

"That's where the unwed deposit them. Poor creature. It's a shame when women like ye so want a child." Mrs. Gretling put a trembling hand to her mouth. She turned and drew the shabby curtains closed. "I didn't mean to remind ye."

The longing, the one that never went away, expanded within Amora's chest and crushed her lungs. Trying to relearn to breathe, she thought of Tomàs as hers, and

Barrington smiling, happy with Amora for giving him a son. She sniffed a bitter portion of air. That day would never come.

"Sorry, Mrs. Norton."

Not wanting her loyal abigail to fret, she schooled her face, forced her dry lips to curl. "Thank you for bringing me."

The old woman's lanky fingers reached for a pale blue blanket from the closet. "Ye seem so happy here, and I know this one is grateful for ye here." Her thick Scottish accent made the abigail's words feel weighty, like ancient wisdom. "We won't see him next week. In the morn, the administrator will send 'im to the wet nurses in the countryside."

"Nothing like fresh air and wide open spaces for children." The Tomàs's orchards, the dark-green wilderness laced with Pippins, that's where she wanted to be now. "What child wouldn't love the country over crowded London?"

"I often think that too."

The masculine voice wasn't as deep as Barrington's, but it still held command. It made her turn toward the door.

A tall man with a wide grin stood at the doorway. The heart-shaped face, the walnut colored eyes. He seemed familiar. "I must go back and get my children," he said. "Just can't bear being in London without them any longer."

Amora tucked the babe deeper into her arms and stared at the intruder. She glanced to Mrs. Gretling. The woman looked charmed, her cheeks turning red.

He plodded inside. His top hat flopped as if it would fall any minute. A cinnamon waistcoat peeked from his dark blue coat and buff breeches. His smudged boots echoed along the floor.

She borrowed strength from her ancestors and drew Tomàs into a deeper, more protective clench. "Do I know you?"

When his hand landed lightly on her elbow, she jumped. "Mrs. Norton, there's nothing to be afraid of. I am Vicar Wilson, and I'm quite good with infants."

The voice. Had she heard it over her screams? Sounds and visions of her miscarriage flooded back into remembrance. The shine of the doctor's sharp knife against her forearm. The smell of iron and wetness. And some smooth hand holding hers, praying for her. The vicar?

She peered up and squinted at him. It was him. He looked better, less scary without fever tainting her vision.

"May I?" The vicar held out his palms. "My boy is just over a year."

There was a softness in his eyes. Something peaceful about the lift of his lips.

She placed Tomàs in the man's arms.

Vicar Wilson started to hum as he adjusted the babe. The tune had something to do with grace, whatever that was.

The little one looked comfortable as his bright blue eyes closed in sleep.

"See, I told you I do well with children. And on Sunday's at St. George's, I practice offering naps to the congregation."

Mrs. Gretling sauntered to him, took the babe, and laid him in the crib. "Mrs. Norton, the vicar is just teasin' about making the church sleep. Haven't put me to sleep yet, nor any of the ladies on Sunday."

A blush crept onto the man's lean features. "Mrs. Gretling, you've made me feel so welcome. I'm grateful. Tuesday's mutton was delicious."

He bent and kissed her hand. He seemed very friendly, maybe too friendly.

Her abigail turned beet red. "I need to go get your shawl, Mrs. Norton. The temperature outside has dropped. Reverend, do keep my lady company?"

"It will be my pleasure." He held the door for Mrs. Gretling. "The babe and I will keep her entertained."

Before she could object, the spry woman was out of the room.

With her gaze settling on the worn floor planks, Amora counted nails heads. Hopefully, Mrs. Gretling wouldn't be long.

His boots pounded. His shadow soon enveloped her, as did the spicy scent of sandalwood. "How are you, Mrs. Norton? I've been most anxious to know."

She took a step backward then gazed at his face. "I am well."

A sigh left him, as if he'd been concerned. "That is good."

She shook her fist at his awful tone. It held nothing but pity. That condescending tone was reserved for Barrington, no one else. "Leave me."

"No, I cannot. The night you miscarried, you said things. Awful things, Mrs. Norton. Things you haven't told anyone, not even your husband."

Amora shrank away until the wall kept her from retreating farther. This stranger knew her secret. "Get away from me."

He stood very still. "I will keep your confidence for now, but you won't know freedom until you tell Mr.

Norton. Have faith in him. All will be well when he knows."

Faith? Faith in God or Barrington? Neither was enough. Neither had or would forgive her. "Mr. Norton has no time for a sick wife. His career cannot be beset with scandals."

"You have to tell him. He needs to know so he can help."

She plucked her gloves from her wristlet reticule. "No. No one else needs to know."

He folded his arms. His sunny disposition cleared. Grim lines, thinned lips, and a cloud of angst covered his face. "I'm going to Hampshire at the end of the week to retrieve my children. In a month, I will return. If I haven't heard from you, I will come to Mayfair and I will tell Mr. Norton that you were abducted."

"You must forget this. I'll lie. Tell him you lie."

"The truth always comes out no matter how carefully constructed the lies or the omissions. Your husband would rather hear the truth from you."

He plodded to the door. "You still suffer from the horror of it. No amount of pretense will take away your pain."

"What if he doesn't believe I was abducted? What if he just thinks that was a lie to cover an affair?"

"I believe you." Vicar Wilson leveled his hat and paced from the room. "Tell him, before it is too late."

What would her husband say, hearing the news from Vicar Wilson or Cynthia?

Her stomach soured. Barrington would hate it. And he'd hate Amora for keeping it secret.

A treacherous jade and a determined minister threatened to destroy her world. Nothing else she valued would be left.

Cynthia could be telling Barrington now. She took a breath and tried to find the right words to tell her husband he'd married a liar.

Amora paced out of her bedchamber into the hall. Her bare feet skimming across the silken weave of the carpet. It wasn't grass, but she felt a little like a hoyden. That's what her mother used to call her because she loved nature, and loved being in nature like her father. When was the last time she danced in the wind or even felt rain on her cheeks?

She stopped at the hall mirror and rubbed her eyes. She wished see saw a hoyden, the independent girl who knew her own mind.

Insides twisting, fighting over what words to use to break Barrington's trust, she went to the window and peered at the lonely street below.

From here, she'd waited hundreds of times to spy Barrington's carriage as soon as it arrived. Then she'd dash down to greet him, hear of his day, and entice him to bed. Having his arms about her kept the monster, most nights, from her dreams. Most nights. On those others, shivering against Barr's sleep warmed form made her realize she was safe and the monster hadn't taken Barrington away either as he promised.

She peaked again at the curtains. Always waiting for Barrington. Waiting for him to claim her hand in a dance at one of Mama's balls. Waiting for him to return from the war. Waiting for him to save her.

With a hand to her brow, she thought past this sorry state, but every sound of a horse's hooves shook her to the core. The truth would be out soon, and the rest of her world would be destroyed.

Maybe that was for the best.

The waiting needed to end.

She tugged at the creamy fabric and took one final look. Nothing but night and stars. What if accepting that he'd never come home again, that he'd abandon her for her deception freed Amora from this sorry state? If she lost everything, could she find herself?

"Ma'am." Mrs. Gretling's voice appeared out of nowhere.

Stopping her shakes, Amora turned. "Yes?"

Her abigail climbed the remaining stairs and now stood on the landing. "Would you like some tea? Something to soothe you? You've been anxious since the hospital."

"I, I'm not thirsty. But, can you tell me if Mr. Norton said he was to be on time?"

Mrs. Gretling wiped her hands on her apron. "It's not yet ten, ma'am."

Her brow shot up as she came closer. "Oh, I should've known not to take ye there yet. I'm sorry. I thought it would be good for you to be out, to be with the children. It usually makes you happy."

Amora cinched her robe. The snowy muslin that hugged her neck seemed to choke her. "I just need to be free... to speak to Mr.–"

The sound of horses' hooves filtered inside. Amora turned to the window and peeked out in time to see Barrington descend from the carriage and head toward the portico. Her heart slowed to a normal rhythm. This was her last chance to tell him. "Inform Mr. Norton that I wish to see him in my chambers."

Creases filled Mrs. Gretling's forehead. "Yes, ma'am."

Amora watched the woman plod down the steps, and then closed her eyes. The fear of Barrington hating her over the truth would be gone. He'd either forgive her or banish her, but at least she'd know and no longer be enslaved to wondering. Only the nightmares of her memories would remain. One source of trepidation had to be better than two. Pulse throbbing, she lifted her chin and plodded to her room. If her marriage must die, it would be with her own hands.

Barrington knocked on Amora's bedchamber then let himself inside. Fumbling with parchment, he took a breath and readied to explain his slight tardiness. "I let the time get away from me pouring through records Beakes located on an old crime. These dates have my head a bit fogged, but I'll be ready for bed once I review this lease for the Dowag..."

Speech robbed, he adjusted his spectacles. His eyes popped wide open at the sight of Amora. A sheer robe draped her long neck. The translucent muslin displayed the lacing of her stays and the flare of her hips beneath a white chemise. His pulse galloped to a higher pace imagining the softness confined beneath.

The papers in his hand fell to the floor. The Dowager's contract would have to fend for itself. "Are you readying for bed?"

She lowered her chin, breaking his stare. "I have to tell you something."

Weeks of sleeping next to Amora, touching but not touching, always abstaining numbered in his head.

Was she ready for that to end?

Did she want him?

He rubbed at his neck, hoping his thoughts would

become coherent or at least not choking on longing. "Amora, tell me what you want?"

"I should've told you a long time ago, but I was afraid."

Not exactly the alluring words he hoped, though she didn't need to do much in this period of physical famine to start his heart pumping. "I'm listening."

The lithe goddess wasn't smiling. "I don't want you to hate me, Barrington."

That definitely wasn't an invitation for bliss, but that didn't mean it couldn't lead to one. He stepped fully inside her bedchamber and closed the door with his heel. His gaze never left her, not even for a second.

She started to pace, making the fabric float about her. Never more alluring, yet she held such a serious pout on her face. What could be the matter? Surely, she couldn't be cross at him. But, she was a woman and her moods changed fast. He drew himself up. Tugging on his lapels, he gazed over his lenses and forced his lips to thin. It was his most contrite and humored look. "Whatever I have done, I'm sorry. Repentant actually. Let me hold you and make amends."

"This is serious."

How was he to listen to anything with her dressed for bed and not bundled up like a mummy. The canopied mattress was five paces from him, maybe three from her stance at the vanity. Oh, what he wouldn't give for a meeting of the minds, bodies, and spirit. He sobered and charged headlong at the problem. "Tell me what makes you frown."

Her bare feet shifted, but her countenance never rose. "I have no peace, it's in my dreams. Vicar Wilson said I should just tell you. He's right."

"The vicar?" Barrington paced to the footboard and allowed his tightened fist to hide behind the knurled pole of the bedframe. "Did he come to Mayfair?"

"No, I saw him on my outing with Mrs. Gretling."

A protective nature was a powerful weapon in Barrington's personal arsenal. It overpowered his senses when it came to Amora. How many noses did he bloody of his fellow soldiers when they taunted him about being faithful to a sweetheart hundreds of miles away? On the day Gerald Miller stepped in front of him, taking a fatal bullet, Barrington had pummeled at least one. Fingers coiling tight like a spring about to burst, he readied for a reason to punch the preacher. "Did the vicar upset you?"

"No, not truly. But he's right in his wisdom." She bit her lip and spun toward the window.

Right about what? "Amora?" His voice sounded too loud, too harsh. Not wanting to provoke an argument when Wilson deserved the censure, he lowered his tone. "Please. It's just you and me here. Tell me what's distressing you."

She shook her head, causing a long dark braid to unravel from her chignon. It fluttered like a flag along her straight posture, down to her waist. Definitely something to pledge allegiance to.

"I didn't tell you, Barr. You deserved to know. You deserved better."

He slid his hands from the canopy and switched his gaze from her satin hair to her curvy hips. Still not a good option if this conversation would lead to continued celibacy. His eyelids shuttered close. He waited for her complaint. "Just say it, Amora."

"A long time ago, eight months before you returned from the Peninsula. I was ..." Her voice shook with sobs.

She sounded as if she were drowning. "It happened."

The urge to save her, to keep her safe in his arms surged in his veins, but he forced his feet to stay put. "I won't argue. I'll accept what you say. I want to make you happy, more than ever. I lov--"

"Abducted." She pivoted, faced him, and finished. "I was abducted."

She moved toward him. Her gait was slow like the world had stopped. His definitely had.

Something dragged on his arm. Was it her palm? He couldn't tell. His gut stung from an unseen punch. He almost doubled over trying to catch a breath. Everything burned. His chest. His lungs. His heart.

"I was abducted, Barr. Say something."

He watched her lips move. Witnessed sighs, the blinking of eyes pregnant with tears, but he couldn't comprehend any of her words beyond *abducted*.

"Barrington, I was. And I hid it in lies."

Abducted, taken, forced. Euphemisms for rape. No, that couldn't be what happened. And Amora wouldn't lie. Not his Amora. "Not true."

She shook her head. His gut knotted, and then broke into pieces.

Abducted.

And she lied.

Lied about something so horrible.

Didn't trust him enough to know the truth.

Didn't love him enough and chose a lie.

Unsteady, he shifted his legs and wobbled to the open side of the bedframe. He sat, more like dropped onto the mattress. Another inch and he'd surely have hit the floor.

She followed and knelt at his side. Her eyes mirrored glass. "Say something. I fear your opinions."

Her fears? That was her concern, not destroying the illusion he believed his life.

"Please, Barr. Tell me your thoughts."

Did the memories of the abduction spurn her nervousness, the questioning if he'd ever come home? Did it send her into a fit that killed their child? He wiped his dry mouth and put a hand over his shriveling heart. "I don't...don't know what to say."

"You're a barrister. Asking questions is in your blood." She rubbed at her temples. "Make this a courtroom. Ask, then judge, then condemn."

Fat droplets rolled down her cheeks. She crossed her arms and hugged herself as if chilled, but the window was closed. "Just do it. I've tortured myself for far too long waiting for this day."

Her words sounded brave. But she trembled.

He'd seen witnesses this scared. They had to be handled with great care. He cupped her ice cold hands and coddled it against his knee. "Tell me what happened."

"I fought him. But he, he str-uck m-me." Her shoulders shook. Her voice rose, terror present in each winded syllable. "My... my fault. Should'a been more careful, more watch--ful."

How could he hear any sordid details with her becoming hysterical? His insides stewed, yet he swallowed his own anger and his questions and gathered her into his arms. "You don't have to say any more. Please calm, my love."

She pulled back and put a shaking palm to his cheek. "Mother said you would hate me if you knew. I can't live with you hating me."

"Never. I could never do that. The war shouldn't have

lasted so long. Even a good girl can be tricked and made vulnerable."

"I wasn't careful. I was so upset over Papa's death. I didn't think."

What exactly was she admitting to? An abduction or a seduction? All afternoon, he'd read account after account of alleged Dark Walk Abductor victims. More than half of the statements weren't credible. A handful, made his skin crawl. The rest, only a jury could decide. Where would his wife's story fall?

Her arms went about his neck. She squeezed so tight. Maybe she thought he'd disappear.

Part of him wanted to. He didn't know her anymore. All these years he believed her faithful. To show her his gratefulness, he'd accepted her mania about his schedule, learned to sleep with candles burning, sent notes of his whereabouts. He'd accepted the leech because he thought she was all his. Lies.

"I wanted to tell you every day, but I didn't know how. I was to protect our love. It's my fault. You have every right to hate me because of this."

Whom had she sought comfort from and became his prey? "Amora, wh—?"

She wove her hands beneath his waistcoat. Her small palms found every muscle tired from stooping over ledgers. "Let me know I haven't ruined things. You hate deception."

"Why tell me now? Not five years ago, when I returned from war?"

"I thought you wouldn't take me as your wife, if you knew. And I needed you to take away the fear. I couldn't lose you. Mama said I would."

What of her overprotective mother? Why hadn't she

watched over Amora?

His nerves jittered like the night before a big trial. Blast it. It was a trial of his manhood and his compassion. She needed him to make everything better. "No more creases under your violet eyes."

With his thumb, he smoothed a tear from her face. Her quiet sobs ripped at what was left of his soul. He'd rather be beat, pummeled, than witness them.

"You've told me, Amora. Now everything will be fine." Did his voice sound even? A thousand questions filled his head but he couldn't be a barrister right now. Just a husband. One desperate to comfort his wife. "All will be well."

"Will it? Things weren't fine before."

True. But maybe his debt of her miscarriage canceled hers over this omission. He needed logic. Nothing in his head felt ordered. Everything swirled out of control pressing him with doubt and grief. Who did it? The faces of every man who ever commented on her beauty flashed into the witness box in his mind. Who abused her?

And did she fancy the rake, even for a moment?

Her robe slipped, exposing the creamy silk of her shoulder. Someone else had seen this loveliness. Someone else had possessed her.

Tracing the curve of her neck, Barrington sought the feel of her to fix the disappointment filling him. "You've told me. This is done. You needn't think of it again tonight."

"Can't think past it anymore."

He whipped off his spectacles, tossing them to the table by the bed. Amora would be able to look into his eyes and see the flames torching his innards over someone hurting her. Or worse, his newly formed doubts about her, about their marriage.

He tucked her head beneath his chin and held her. Maybe the Lord would smother the fire lighting his bones. Probably wouldn't since he and God hadn't communicated since the miscarriage. It was up to Barrington alone to make things better.

Minutes, maybe an hour passed. Her cries died down. She lifted from his embrace. "Well, I've said it. I've finally told you." She moved a couple inches away and put a foot on the floor. "You can go work now."

He wasn't going to be dismissed and leave this thing, the omission, and the other man, to remain a gulf between them. Wrenching out of his waistcoat, he wrapped his arms about her, kissing that spot along her throat until she released a raspy giggle.

She curled her fingers about his cravat. "Barr, you forgive me?"

He nodded quickly. He didn't know what to say when he wanted to break bricks. Some fiend took advantage of her. His girl. His betrothed. Why couldn't the war have ended sooner so he could've protected her? Maybe he shouldn't have enlisted at all. Grandfather would have been disappointed, but he could have stayed at her side.

"You still want me? Mama was wrong?"

A tremor set in his jaw at the fear in her voice. His blasted pharaoh want-to-be mother-in-law. The tenuous reign on his emotions snapped. "You are mine, Amora. No matter what."

He lifted her to him and took her mouth. Gentle at first. Soft, so she could send him away. She leaned into him.

Tugging at her robe, he pushed the muslin down her

arms. With his record-indexing finger, he hooked the ribbon in her hair and shook free her locks. Raven colored silk now draped her buttermilk skin.

This is how she'd looked on their wedding night. Eyes large, shining in the candlelight, waiting for what he'd do next.

Why wasn't he the first to behold her?

And the only one. How could he not have known?

Pride battered, he claimed her mouth again. Maybe their union now would assure her of his forgiveness and obscure all memories of others.

Maybe it would reassure him too that she was still his.

With one arm, he pushed away the bedclothes from the firm mattress below.

Nails stroking his shoulder, she found that spot on his back, the tender muscle that could be scored with her name. She didn't want to be freed, and he wouldn't let her go.

Her lips trembled beneath his. With a taste to her cheek, tears salted his tongue, seasoning the desire arcing inside. It had to be his name in her kiss, in her dreams, in her memories.

He sought every part of her, branding her with fevered hands. Descending upon her, Barrington kissed her until both gasped for air.

Chapter Six: Covering Darkness

Amora opened her eyes to slits. Complete darkness surrounded her. Shivering, she wanted to close them again, but she couldn't. She had to know where she was. And where Barrington was too.

She moved her feet against the bedsheets. Sheets meant Mayfair, her home with Barrington.

Releasing a tight breath, she relaxed her coiled muscles a smidge. How to be sure? Filling her lungs to capacity, she shot up and grabbed the heavy silver candleholder from the bed table and swung in the chilly air.

Nothing was there.

She eased her weapon to the table then dropped to the mattress. Her candle had burnt out. Nothing more sinister. Letting the moonlight stream through the window, she fingered her matches and lit the stubby candle.

Her bedchamber, the grey walls, the sturdy white painted furnishings, all came into focus. Heart light, she rolled onto her side to snuggle next to Barrington's sleep warmed form, but the bed was empty. Pulling the bed sheets up to her chin, she caught the scent of him, a pleasant mix of starch and rainwater.

He must've gotten up to work. Very odd for him to do so and not make sure her candle was lit.

But Barrington may have other things on his mind. Her lip curled up releasing the glow flowing in her heart.

She'd told him.

And he still loved her.

Barrington was a good man, a good lover. Caring, thoughtful, nothing like the womanizing husbands of her cousins. But tonight, he was different. Unrestrained, maybe even out-of-control, not Barrington.

His searing kisses made her feel more than treasured, more than safe. He needed her. It had been a long time since he'd been desperate to touch her.

She fingered the outline of his empty space. This was a new beginning. They'd found each other again. She couldn't let his work separate them.

Popping up, she scooped on her robe. With her candle in hand, she set out for him. The house lay dark and quiet. Her eyes adjusted. She felt secure with her candle's glow. Feet still bare, she traipsed down the stairs and turned toward his study.

A small light came from his sealed door.

She opened it and found a chilly room with her poor husband slumped at his desk. His tanned brow contrasting the white parchment and foolscap stacked about his head.

Should she wake him? Would he begin asking questions she couldn't answer? Who did abducted her? Where did he drag her too?

He'd been so kind and understanding, but his thirst for

truth overpowered at times. Maybe they could search for them together.

With Barrington still loving her, his strength would keep the memories from consuming her, wouldn't it?

Courage faltering, she almost pivoted. But she couldn't leave him, not in this cold. His hip would ache. Being shot dragging his best friend's body out of the path of the enemy was something he didn't talk much about, but she knew he kept it in his heart everyday.

Pattering to the hearth, she stoked the ashes. The dark gray and onyx char reminded her of charcoal sketches. For a moment, the poker was flint. She feathered along the grate. Maybe tomorrow she could make Barrington something.

With a shake, she stopped woolgathering and pushed coals together. Their orange heat expanded and warmed the next lump. She dumped on a log. It sparked, then smoked, and finally caught. The hearth just needed tending. Maybe their marriage worked like that. With her deception cleared, the coals of their love could be stoked again. Smiling inside, she put a couple of logs in the fireplace.

"Amora." His voice heavy with sleep reached her ears. She pivoted to him, but his face held stern lines.

"Go back to bed, sweetheart."

"I wanted to see about you." She lifted her hand to him. "Come with me."

He didn't move. The blank look in his grey eyes cut through her.

"I've a little more work to do. Go on, Amora. Return to your chambers."

With his need for passion sated, was she of no use to him? The idea of them working together faded away.

Her arms pimpled, but not from the cold. Those embraces meant good bye. She'd lost him. His heart was dead to her. Nodding, she rushed to the door.

"I'll be up soon."

No, he wouldn't. Work was his first love. Now maybe his only. "Take your time."

On the other side of his door, she restrained herself from ramming her head. Her husband's pity was not needed. There was enough flowing from her own soul.

Barrington swiped at his forehead. It wasn't particularly warm in the Old Bailey's courtroom today, but his thoughts blazed. In fact, if he wasn't careful, he'd scorch his horsehair wig.

Order your thoughts, man. Difficult to do when out there in the world lived another man who tricked Amora.

Discipline, man. Pretend Grandfather watched. In a few minutes, the verdict would be rendered. Had he done enough to defend his client to absolve him of theft?

Half-listening would fail most. Luckily, Barrington wasn't most. Not when it came to the law. Yet, he must be a terrible man if his wife couldn't confide in him. Amora hadn't trusted his commitment, or she would have admitted the truth much earlier. Always working for others, perhaps he'd given her reasons to doubt his dedication to her and their marriage. Lord knows her miscarriage indicted him.

Her words echoed in his ear, 'I was abducted'.

He grabbed the table leg of the barrister's bench and imagined placing his palms about the neck of the man who had treated her so shamefully. Who did it?

Could he forget it, being five years too late? Amora had.

But had she? The fear of the dark, was it from her attacker? Always needing to know where Barrington was, was that too from the fiend? Or was it in the hopes of keeping Barrington in the dark? What else did she have to hide?

And the way she dressed last night. Sheers, ruffles, textures that heightened his senses, his awareness of her. Was it all to manipulate him?

He cracked his knuckles as the crowd in the courtroom laughed and hooted. He released his hold on the desk, but couldn't focus.

Amora kept this dreadful secret and the villain never paid for hurting her.

Unless there was no villain.

A willing participant in a seduction would make for no crime. What was the truth? Was that why she couldn't tell Barrington?

Exhaling, he wiped the moisture beading upon his brow. No more thoughts of what can't be changed. He told Amora the *abduction* was in the past. Now, he needed to convince himself.

"Norton, are you well?" Hessing leaned closer. His onion-laced breath fouled the air.

"I'm well." He pivoted in time to watch Lord Justice Burns hit his gavel against his desk. The elegant sleeves of his court silks billowed with each pound. "Take a moment, jurymen, and consider your verdict."

Silence fell upon the crowd.

For once, Barrington wished he could see the crimson color of the robe. From all accounts, the hue spoke of power, and the Lord Justice knew how to use it.

The man leaned forward toward the jurymen. "What is the verdict?"

The lead juror leapt up and straightened his waistcoat. "Not guilty, Lord Justice."

The crowd erupted as the bailiff stepped forward and unchained Barrington's client.

"Winner." Hessing tapped his shoulder. "Join me for dinner at my club, Norton. I'd like to discuss a case with you, one dealing with an old crime. It involves murder."

"There's no time limit on murder." From the corner of his eye, Barrington spied Cynthia Miller waving to him from the gallery. "Sir."

A chortle bubbled from Hessing. "I see why you've been distracted, Norton. Sly fox." The man leaned forward as his gaze seemed set on the pretty songstress in a tight blue gown. Its bodice was incredibly low. I'll be at my club, if you get your hands free." His mentor chuckled and left the courtroom.

Barrington paced up the stairs. He didn't like Hessing thinking of Cynthia as a doxy. Though her choice of outfits needed more thought, she was Gerald's little sister. Someone who needed to be protected in her brother's absence.

Cynthia lifted her hand to him, but he avoided clasping it.

Instead, he folded his arms. No need to stoke gossip. He was a married man with a spotless reputation. Others might not think too kindly of such a fair woman warming to a mulatto. Barrington knew his limitations in society. "What are you doing here?"

Cocking back her head, she pouted. Her lips thinned to a child-like frown. "You haven't answered any of my correspondences or come to one of my reviews."

He leaned back on the knee wall of the gallery. "I've been very busy."

With a light stroke, she patted his arm. "You're mad at me. I meant no harm to Mrs. Norton. How was I to know she'd get upset and jump from my carriage?"

He cut his gaze to her. She leapt backwards as if she bled. "She didn't mention this. What made her upset?"

She swiveled her long neck and waved to an admiring gentleman or two. "I'd rather not say here."

Another of Amora's secrets. Yet, knowing the ladies fought wouldn't change things. He couldn't hold Cynthia responsible for his child's fate. The fault was his, for not being home to calm Amora down. For believing God cared enough to intervene.

A huff left his lips. "Come. Follow me to a witness room."

Down the stairs and to the right, he led her out of the courtroom through the hall to a small room. Once inside, he shut the door. Pulling off his wig and barrister's collar, he sat on the table's edge. "Miss Miller, I am very busy. Why are you here? I suspect it is not another theater invitation."

Again with a pout, and this time tears, she approached. "But you've always made time for me."

"Things are different. For some reason, you upset my wife. Could you tell me why?"

She pivoted and sashayed in front of the window. "What did Amora say?"

The urge to close the beige curtains to obscure onlookers from viewing the two of them pressed at his gut. He rubbed his brow. "This is my decision. I have to better prioritize my time."

"No, this is her doing. She hates me, just because I mentioned telling you of her disappearance."

Cynthia knew of the abduction? Her angelic looking

face seemed to harden. Something in her squinting eyes looked vengeful. Why?

Barrington took off his court silk and tried to appear aloof. "She didn't mention an incident in your carriage, but why don't you tell me what you know of her disappearance. You seem eager to say."

Her eyes went wide as if she'd expected a different reaction. She dug into her reticule and pulled out a handkerchief. "I just know of the gossip. That she disappeared for one or two months. But she wants you to believe she waited for you like a saint."

A month? Not a day or two. His throat became dry like a desert, one scorched by lies. Years of training kept his countenance even. Cynthia didn't need to see the venom building in his muscles. Forgetting became impossible. He had to know the name of the blackguard who ran away with Amora, an engaged woman. "Do you know where she went? With whom?"

A tiny smile crept onto her face, but quickly disappeared. "No one knows. But I suspect it was one of the Charleton brothers." Her sweet tone took on haughty airs. "Both visited the Tomàs Orchards a great deal in your absence."

The dowager's sons? The earl of Clanville? Or his younger brother, the rake Charleton? Which one had hurt Amora?

"Did she mention that?" Bosom heaving, Cynthia leaned over the table. She was putting on quite a show, if someone were interested.

He lifted his gaze to the window and hid his balling fists beneath his silk. He was a respected barrister not a young buck ready to bloody every nose.

Cynthia put a hand on his shoulder. "But I need help.

It's dire."

"What?"

She launched into his arms. So quick was the action, her straw bonnet fell away. Her chignon unraveled.

His fingers tangled in the stiffness of the locks. "What is it, woman?"

Cynthia clung to the lapels of his waistcoat. Fear laced her musical voice. "It's Gerald."

"What about your brother?"

She started to cry. "He's alive and in trouble."

Nothing would be better than for the man who saved his life to be alive, but it wasn't possible. Barrington pushed free. "What type of joke is this?"

"It's not a joke. He is alive."

His voice strangled. Anger wrapped and crushed his windpipe like a hangman's noose. "Gerald Miller is deceased. I was there when he was shot. He took a bullet meant for me."

"Did you see his last breath?" Sobs mixed with her words. "Did you watch them bury him?"

"No, the surgeon was pulling lead out of my hide." His heart ached for his lost friend. What he wouldn't give for this to be true? But it wasn't. "Cynthia, I will take care of this."

"Oh, Barrington." She kissed his cheek and tried to weave her arms about his waist.

He moved her hands and tilted her chin up. "I will find this pretender and turn the fiend over to the runners. He'll never bother you with these lies again."

"No. You mustn't. Gerald is alive, but he'll hang for what they accuse him of." She pulled away and dashed out the room.

Some blackguard had convinced her he was Gerald.

Another evil man attempted to hurt a woman, one under his protection. He couldn't save Amora from her fiend. Someone she ran away with for two months. But he'd stop this one. Barrington would make sure the blackguard paid dearly, either through the courts or fisticuffs.

The sound of a creaking board forced a tremor up her spine. Amora wasn't alone in the pitch blackness. She stood and rammed into a wall. Clutching her knees, she sank deeper into the dark corner. No breathing, just hoping the monster hadn't heard her.

"Hello."

The muffled voice tried to coax her out of hiding. She willed her heart to beat slower. If she stayed hidden, he wouldn't touch her, not hurt her as he did Sar...

Her temples throbbed. Her lost friend's name sat on her tongue, but she couldn't remember any more of it.

She rubbed the vacant spot on her pinkie finger where Papa's ring once sat and tried to conjure up a plan. Something brave, worthy of the Tomàs blood flowing within her veins.

Thump. Thump. Boot heels stopped seven, no six paces away.

Pulse racing, she fingered the smooth wall hoping to pry loose a plank.

"Amora?"

Evil knew her name.

The hushed tone sent shivers flooding her skin. She pivoted, reached up and clasped the edge of a heavy flat object. Cold, stone.

"Stay back!" Her voice cracked. The intended warning sounded like a cat's purr.

The large shadow came closer.

She started hurling things--sticks, discs. Anything, she could fit within her palms. In the blackness, she couldn't discern the objects, but he wouldn't hurt her like the others, not without a fight.

"Stop it, Amora."

The swish of a match strike sounded and set a wall sconce ablaze.

She squinted as a cold hard knot filled her middle.

Barrington scraped at the gravy clinging to his jacket, chestnut brown on his stark onyx tailcoat. "What has gotten into you?"

Light-headed, Amora rose from her corner and scanned the littered dining room. A spent candleholder and smashed fruit covered the mahogany hardwoods. Splattered walls framed Barrington's 6' 2" limbs. The pale silver paper treatment now bore drippy dark splotches. A piece of potato slipped down to the floor like an oozing snail.

Barrington shook his head and pivoted away from the long table to yank the bell pull.

Mayfair. She was at Mayfair, their London townhome. A puff of relief fled her mouth as she tugged on the itchy neck frill of her gown.

"Answer me." The measured tone contrasted with his tight grip on his collar. He stripped off the tailcoat but even his cravat held stains. A portion of his short cut charcoal colored hair held a dollop of potatoes. He brushed it out with his wrist. "Amora?"

"Sorry." She rounded the dining table and rushed toward him. With a napkin from their spoiled dinner, she sponged his shoulder. "I thought you were ..."

"A burglar?" He grimaced. "I come home late and this

is what I get."

Balling the cloth, she reached up and wiped the tip of his nose. Splatter even dotted his spectacles. Yet the plains of his face were smooth, seemingly devoid of emotion. Where was the man who held her yesterday as if he were desperate for her love?

The monster took that too.

What was next, her sanity?

Her eyes stung. "The candle must've gone out while I waited for you."

He wrenched the napkin away. Noisy air fled his nostrils.

His lips pressed together as he thumbed a smear of brown from his cheek. "I understand. All is well."

How could it be? She looked down at the cluttered floor. The sketch she made from spent coal ash, the first drawing in years laid in a pile of broken plates. Destroyed, ruined like their dinner, she couldn't give it to Barrington now.

He must be so tired of her excuses, her nightmares. She sighed. She was tired too.

Barrington lifted her chin. "Was it another dream about the two months you were abducted?"

How did he know how long? She hadn't told him.

He pulled her closer. "You can tell me. I won't judge you."

Chrysanthemum scent hovered in his cravat and along his waistcoat. The tart, Cynthia Miller had been in his arms, whispering her sordid gossip.

Bunching up her collar, she backed away. He went from loving Amora straight to Cynthia. Did they compare notes and laugh at her?

How foolish she was to believe things would change by

telling him the truth. Everything had become worse. His wife, the liar, was enough to send him to willing arms.

He scooped wasted vegetables and beefsteaks onto a shard of the broken Wedgewood. His knuckles tightened about the fragment as if he hid anger. "Well if not tonight, then, when you are ready."

With a shrug, she stepped behind Barrington away from the strong arms that should enwrap her and chase away her fear. No, she couldn't admit to being scared and give additional fodder to his mistress confidante. She stooped and picked up broken plates.

Mrs. Gretling marched inside wearing her tartan robe, her graying auburn hair filled with curl papers. "What happened here?"

The housekeeper neared on all fours and took the sharp pieces of china from Amora. Her soft cherry eyes misted. "Don't hurt yourself, Mrs. Norton. I'll have this all cleaned up. Nothing like a good sleep to set things right."

The portly woman was so protective. But nothing would set things right, ever.

Barrington neared and lifted Amora to her feet. "Rest. I'll assist the housekeeper."

What could she say after pummeling him with beefsteak, and him smelling like chrysanthemums? She nodded and slipped from the room.

In the quiet hall, she leaned against the wall and watched the flicker of cranberry colored flames fluttering in a sconce.

James plodded at the end of the corridor lighting others. He stopped in front of her and lit the one over her head.

Within a blink, wonderful light showered her.

"Ma'am, if I'd known you had something special planned I would have gotten him home." The burly man bowed his head as if the floor was more interesting than the crazy woman who'd just caused another disaster for his employer.

He glanced up, "I would've done that."

His face, ruddy with flecks of henna along his jaw where a beard might grow, glowed in the brightness of the hall. His hair was ebony but hidden beneath the colored powder Barrington had him wear. It was such an old tradition, just like Grandfather Norton's servants. Yet, James never complained. He bore it all with grace.

He fingered his silver blue livery and straightened his posture. "Do you need anything?"

Nothing that even faithful James could fix. "I've made quite a muddle in the dining room." She pivoted to the stairs. The second level appeared dark and foreboding.

"Wait, Mrs. Norton." He placed a candle in her hand. "I haven't had a chance to light the upstairs yet. This will guide you."

Something, maybe understanding, simmered in his deep chocolate eyes.

"Thank you. I like the light." She took a step and held onto the railing.

"You have to do more than just like it. You have to seek it, fight for it to be in your life."

She pivoted and stared at him. Could James understand suffering? "I've no fight left."

"Ma'am?" James's strong voice made her blink and grip the stairs more firmly. "Should I get Mr. Norton?"

With a shake of her head, she charged up the rest of the stairs. Her eyes were too full of water to turn and say goodnight.

With Mrs. Gretling and James tidying up the dining room, Barrington trudged up the stairs to find his wife. He stripped off his fouled waistcoat, swiped a spot of gravy from his ear lobe and put it to his mouth. A hint of garlic and onions danced on his tongue. His wife had prepared his favorite, smothered beefsteaks. Pity it sat in Mrs. Gretling's rubbish bin.

Huffing air through his tight lips, he stood at Amora's sealed door and fingered the panels.

Ordinarily, he might've thought she acted out of anger, but the scowl on her countenance possessed wide eyes. Her skin felt clammy. She looked lost, frightened, very frightened. A waking nightmare?

He traced the door knob. Maybe tonight she would tell him she'd run off with a rake for over a month then changed her mind when Barrington arrived late.

From all the evidence, Amora's behavior and Cynthia's testimony, that had to be what happened. A sigh fled his lung's empty soul. What else had she not told him?

Wanton Intimacy?

A child borne of lust? Or another one lost?

No more staring at the wood like a witless fool. Answers were in the bedchamber. He shoved open her door.

"Barrington?" Amora bounced up from the floor. "I didn't expect you. You never visit when you are unhappy with me."

His old gut twisted again at the loneliness in her voice. His heart slumped bringing his shoulders too. "I wanted to see if you were well."

"I am." Her foot pattered near a candle set on the

ground. What was she planning? To burn the house down?

No, she wasn't crazed. And the woman had never done anything out of spite. Not even throw food.

Waxy smoke filled his nostrils as he bent, picked up the candle, and set it on the bed table. "You don't need to be fearful or uneasy. I'm not mad any more, but is there more I need...to do?" The words, *more I need to know*, stung his tongue but he just couldn't offer them. He needed to take her away some place remote and safe. Somewhere he could absorb the whole of the sordid affair and figure out how to fix their marriage.

She counted her fingers. "I'll be better for the Dowager's ball. You'll be able to depend upon me, but let me be tonight. I need to be alone."

He'd forgotten about his patroness's event. He rubbed his brow. "You do know we can disagree without you looking as if everything were ruined between us."

"I suppose I am to be as accommodating with the things you do wrong." She pushed at her brow. "I just need to sleep. Good night, Barrington."

"You truly want me to leave? That is so unlike you. You usually need me to be about."

A loud sniff sounded. She mated her fingers together. "I realize now why you have to be alone."

The fear in her eyes had disappeared. It was replaced by something he couldn't determine. It felt lonely and dry. His own throat clogged. He had to look away. "Good night. Think no more of the beefsteaks. Thank you again for the kindness of it."

He popped outside and fled to the safety of his study. Something was changing between them. She was too upset to say, and tonight he lacked the strength to inquire.

How could he ask what else she'd hid from him? Did she only marry him to cover her shame?

James came through the door. His gray livery bore perfect creases, amazing after scraping up the Norton's meal. "Is everything well?"

"As well..." Barrington ran a hand through his hair. "See if Mrs. Gretling needs anything."

"Sir, I think..." The man buttoned his lips.

Sinking into his well-worn chair, Barrington waved. "Go ahead. Say your peace."

"You're not fine. Neither is Mrs. Norton."

But what could be done? Barrington swiped at his spectacles. "All incidents are to be forgotten. Make sure my evening coat is pressed. The dowager's ball is tomorrow."

"And Mrs. Norton? You will have her accompany you to an event she takes no pleasure in?"

"My wife should be at my side. It's part of the gift of marriage. For better or worse." This must be the *worse* part. "I'm not in the mood for a lecture, James."

His man yanked out the Bible hidden under the stacks of paper. "When was the last time you sought direction for anything?"

The book splashed open. Creased pages, dog-eared sections lay before him on the clear part of his desk. A few months ago, reading and worshiping started his routine. Now it just reminded him of loss, of failing Amora.

As if just touching the delicate leaves would singe his skin, he leaned back as far from the Bible as possible. "You shepherd me from appointment to appointment. You know my schedule. I've been very busy."

"The missus. She has a haunted look in her eyes, just like the injured militia I tended to coming back from the war. Something dark torments her."

Guilt over her faithlessness. Over a month gone with a rake. His heart ached as if it had just happened, but this wound was five years ago, in the past. He pushed at his brow. "She's never been to war."

"Not your war, but something just as dark." James dipped his head. "Something evil."

"Well, you've said what you needed to say." Barrington reached into his desk for a quill and a bottle of ink. After jotting down a set of instructions, he offered the cut of foolscap. "Take this note to my solicitor early in the morning. I need him to have Miss Miller followed. She's afoot in something truly evil happening now. At least I can protect her."

"Yes, sir." James tucked the folded paper into his jacket. He lingered a moment, then pulled a silver tray from behind his back. A single piece of stationery lay on it. "This was spared."

The fragrance of burnt wood filtered from the page. Bringing it near, the lines of gray and black became clear. It was a sketch of a nightingale. A little smudged, edged with gravy, but beautiful. Barrington's heart pounded hard. "You found this? Where?"

"On the floor next to your seat. I think Mrs. Norton made it for you."

She'd started to sketch again. This would be the first time he'd seen anything of Amora's since he left to fight in the Peninsula. The hollow feeling in Barrington's chest deepened. His being late and her awakening in the dark gave her nightmares. Would it make her avoid the arts again?

"Goodnight." James lumbered through the threshold and shut the door.

Barrington exhaled. He opened a drawer and rummaged inside until he found the original sketch. The beautiful drawing she made for him, memorializing their first kiss.

He held the two images side by side. The new one favored the older one, but felt more somber. The eyes of the bird were vacant, with large soulless pupils. A difference of years. A difference in attitudes.

Barrington pounded his skull, anger at himself boiled over. Stewing over Cynthia's testimony about Gerald and Amora's two months away, he wasn't ready to come home. He chose to go with Hessing to discuss the law. All to avoid being where he was needed, where he should've been.

The sketches floated down from his palm, landing on the open Bible. He'd let Amora down, just like the night of the miscarriage.

And again God was nowhere to be found.

Chapter Seven: No, Not Ready to Party

Amora paced inside her bedchamber. The Dowager Clanville's ball. How would she and Barrington endure it?

The satin of her slippers puckered about her toes as she spun and headed back to the window. The ride to the dowager's house might last an hour. What would she say? Another sorry just seemed tired, like wasted air. Well, maybe it would be his turn to say those words. Would he admit to an affair with Cynthia?

And if he did, what would she do? If she were her mother, Henutsen Tomàs, he'd be shot clean through. Amora rubbed her temples remembering her mother's temper and her accuracy with weapons.

She shook herself, hopefully forcing reason to rattle and show itself within her head. Cynthia's perfume didn't mean an affair, just that he'd seen her. Knowing the singer, she'd find ways to hang on to him just to leave her scent like a skunk.

Amora would make amends by being a perfect wife at this ball. The music and the gentle candlelight, dancing with Barrington…these things should keep her spirits high. James said to seek the light. A well lit ballroom could be the answer.

She folded her arms and slumped against the window. That wasn't what the good man-of-all-work meant.

Seeking light. Why? The Anglican's god hadn't forgiven her. Crying out against Him for taking Papa equaled an abduction. Not telling Barrington before they married equaled the loss of their child. When would her debts be canceled?

Sunday church service would be at the end of the week. Maybe those candles lighting the pews would work. Could Barrington's god offer a truce and not take anything else away?

Better yet, maybe Barrington will forget to go, like last week. It seemed as if he'd been finding ways to miss church. She wondered why.

Maybe she should seek out her mother's gods. Didn't nature take care of her, even feed her in evil's clutches? That would be Geb's domain, since he was god of the earth. Mother said his idols were wise and caring. Surely better to her than Papa's and Barrington's god. And Geb loved his goddess wife.

The knock at her door made her jump.

She steadied her hand along her simple pearl necklace and strengthened her voice. "Come in."

Barrington sauntered inside, elegant as ever in his fine onyx coat and white stockings. He stopped and gazed at her.

Hopefully, she looked well. She was wearing his favorite of her summer dresses, a light blue gown with plenty of lace on its bodice, and beading on the neckline.

"You look lovely." His hand went to his neck.

Why did he already don his hat? "When did you get home? I didn't see you arrive."

His gaze lowered. He picked at lint on his sleeve. "I've been here for a couple hours. I've been thinking about tonight. I don't want you unhappy or under strain."

"I'm *sorry* about last night." The s word grated her nerves.

He stepped close, bent and gave her a peck on the cheek. "You don't like these crowded events, so you don't have to go."

What? She hugged his waist, gripping him tightly. Joy warmed her insides. "We are staying in. Oh, Barrington. This is wonderful."

He pulled her hands away. The smile on his face disappeared, replaced by a tight line that formed on his lips. "No, I'm still attending. I know how miserable they make you and I don't want you burdened."

He meant to leave without her. She retreated and clasped her arms. "I don't understand. We always go to the Dowager's dinners."

"The woman depends upon me. Between her and my colleagues, the conversation about politics and trials, I won't be able to spend much time with you. Why should you fret when you can be safe at home?"

Pain struck her heart. This was about last night. "I won't throw the dowager's plates." She covered her mouth. That came out too harshly. "I won't bring shame upon you in public. I promise."

"I'm trying to be considerate and still meet our social obligations." He came near and lifted her chin. "Next week, I'm going to free my schedule. We'll travel to Cornwall."

She squinted, staring into his blank gray irises. Could

he be serious? No work. No Cynthia. "Cornwall, where we had our wedding trip?"

"Yes. If I can arrange the same rooms, I will."

There were lines under his eyes. He seemed dour, anxious. She couldn't tell what he thought, but something wasn't right.

"Why, now? I've asked for us to go away a dozen times."

He stroked a loose curl from her chignon. "I want you to be relaxed. Perfectly calm and safe, like you were when we wed. Then you'll be able to tell me everything about your disappearance. I have to know. Maybe your nightmares will arrest if you share all the details.

"Everything about the abduction? All that I can remember?"

A brow popped up. He stepped away. "Yes, I need to know it. Once you tell me about the disappearance, we can put it behind us and come back united."

Why did he keep saying *disappearance* as if she hid as in a child's game? Her limbs shook as anger twisted her insides. She vanished but not by choice. Did Barrington not believe her?

He pulled her into his arms and snuggled her against the damask silk of his waistcoat. The shiny ivory buttons brushed her lips.

"All will be forgiven then, beefsteaks, beaus, everything." He kissed her forehead and pivoted to the door. "Don't wait up."

He left. She sank onto the chair next to her vanity. She should be happy not have to endure the thick crowds of the ball, but her fist closed. Barrington doubted her abduction. He didn't trust her anymore, especially in public.

Amora leaned her cheek on the cold glass. Three days ago, he held and kissed her, loved her as if they were beginning anew. Now what would she do? How long before he sent her away? Maybe that was what this trip was about? Mama was right. Barrington hated her because of the truth.

Going home to Mama was not something to wish upon an enemy. There was no place for her, and she couldn't be one of those wives who averted their eyes to their husband's dalliances for baubles. Defeated, she closed her eyes.

An hour or so later, Mrs. Gretling sauntered inside. "Ma'am, why ye still here? The master left some time ago. You're not feeling well again?"

Sitting up straight, Amora took a slow breath. Appear normal, that's what Mother would say to do. She pressed at the crease stamped on her cheek by the edge of vanity. "Can you help me out of this gown?"

Her abigail dropped the blankets she carried and folded her arms. "What are ye doing? Ye are his wife. Ye have to maintain a public face or every evil woman will try to stake a claim on Mr. Norton, including the songstress."

"My husband is in control of his actions." So unlike his wife. She tugged at one of the pins holding the tight twists of her curls.

Mrs. Gretling plodded near and pushed the pin back into the thick folds of her hair. "Ye have to go, ma'am."

Amora pressed her temple. She wasn't wanted, marked by incomplete memories past and lies. "He doesn't want me."

She put a hand to her lips. "So *sorry*..."

"Don't give up. Show him ye will fight for this

marriage. Be his wife in private and in public."

"What are you talking about?"

The woman plodded to the closet and yanked out gray and pale gowns. "Ye've given up colors for him. Ye fret about disappointing him. Ye're dancing on eggshells. It's not good."

Mrs. Gretling neared and picked up the lacy shawl from the bed. "Ye have fire, Mrs. Norton. To toss a beefsteak across the room, ye got it."

She took Amora's hands. "It's in yer veins, but ye've been putting it to sleep. Yer mother says you're in line to the Pharaohs. Be your own Moses and free yourself. Maybe if ye let ye self be free, the nightmares wouldn't come anymore."

How could she regain his respect if she wilted all the time? She stood from the vanity and tugged on her gloves. "What if he orders me to go?"

Mrs. Gretling draped the shawl about Amora's shoulders. "I will be waiting outside. Even the short appearance will stop any rumors. And the master cares too much about what people say to do that. He'll know not to take ye for granted. Show him the Pharaoh in ye."

Proud like Mama? No, proud like Papa. He never hid, and if his life hadn't been stolen, he would have stopped the gossip. Together they would have walked through the village of Clanville with heads held high. He'd believed her, without question.

She'd go, not for Barrington, but for Papa. He didn't raise a Tomàs who hid from battle, one without fire. The girl who fought the monster couldn't be gone.

Barrington bent his head and talked more nonsense to some chattering miss. From witnessing Cheshire's disappointment to reliving his argument with Amora, he couldn't focus. No records of port had been located. The duke wasn't happy, and his devotion to finding answers for his duchess was palatable. New love was best.

Dying love was the worst. It dwarfed every thought and made every insecurity a man could possess grow.

Amora's frown saddened him. Excusing her from attending the Dowager's ball should've made her happy, but it didn't. Why couldn't he please her?

The wail of the violin drowned the young lady's dribble about a play or did she mention Prinny. Something with a P.

He'd never been so distracted. Months of planning for a son dashed and now this *abduction* business.

Who was the man with whom Amora disappeared? What did she mean, *what she could remember*? Getting her to admit the truth had to happen as soon as possible, or he might start having nightmares and throwing beefsteaks.

The thought that she might've fancied anyone else enough to run away with them stabbed at his vanity. His heart had been broken with her lie, so vanity was all he had left. It needed to be protected.

Trying to laugh at himself had become more difficult. The feeling of losing was difficult for a winning barrister. But Barrington wasn't stupid. He was losing Amora and he didn't know why.

Could the nightmares be bringing back her love for the man she ran away with? The affair turned dark, enough to traumatize her. There had to be something keeping her in bondage. Guilt couldn't account for all her fears, the unease in her spirit.

He released a strong sigh. No matter how it began,

there was a blackguard out in the world who needed to be beaten to edge of his life for hurting Amora.

"Mr. Norton? Mr. Norton?" The blonde tapped his folded arms. "You haven't stated your preference?"

Oh, a nod wouldn't do. He relaxed his forearm, dragging them behind his back. "The first?"

"I knew you liked the theater." She smoothed the tufted sleeve, an indeterminate color of green or blush. Nothing like the blue Amora wore.

She looked so beautiful in his favorite of her gowns. The contrast of the lace trimming the pleats in her bodice and the slick sarcenet always made his fingers tingle. Maybe she could wear it to Cornwall. Maybe they could begin again. Could he truly forgive her?

Whatever the truth, an abduction or a scandalous seduction, he needed to know. James was right. Until things were resolved, dragging her to these events would not be well.

Barrington timed his exit from the chattering miss to the end of the musician's set and headed for air.

As he pressed on the balcony doors, the strains of an argument filtered through the crack. The sharp tones soon blended with the start of a pianoforte.

Barrington craned his ear. Who could so openly find disagreement at the Dowager's ball? He peeked through the curtains.

Cynthia stood there waving her hands, swatting a tall gentleman who stood in the shadows. He gripped her wrists and then tugged them to her sides.

No one manhandles a woman. Barrington shoved open the door.

The fellow dropped her arms. Cynthia came running to Barrington. Tears began to trickle down her cheeks.

The fiend came into the light. It was Mr. Charleton, the dowager's younger son, the womanizer.

Stepping to the door, he tugged on his patterned waistcoat and leaned close to Barrington's ear. "Don't fall for the waterworks, old boy. The wench can cry on demand."

"Never put your hands on her or any other." He put an arm about Cynthia to steady her, then lowered his voice. "Do you understand, Charleton?"

"I know better than to lay with snakes. You should smarten up, too." He trudged back into the ballroom, closing the doors behind him.

"Miss Miller, did he hurt you?"

"No." She swiped at her eyes.

"Then what was this about? You didn't go to him about *Gerald*, asking for help for the impostor?"

She pulled away and pushed at the tendrils falling from her braided chignon. "Well, I need someone to take me seriously."

He took what she said very seriously. When the investigators discovered the man's location, Barrington would personally take care of the problem. "You know Charleton is a rake. I've drafted many settlements for the dowager to cover his by-blows."

"Good." Her lips pushed out. Her breath sputtered.

"Someone needs to pay for those poor children. Then one of those mothers might keep her child and not wonder every day of what became of her. I look at every little red-haired girl of seven or eight and wonder if she's mine."

As she plodded to the stone barrier of the balcony, Cynthia's shoulders shook. Quiet tears flowed, glistening in the moonlight. The girl seemed in agony.

His gut twisted. The pain of losing his own child, all the plans he had for his son washed through him. A tremble began in his balled fists. *God, I would've been a dependable father, nothing like the rake Charleton or my own.*

He came near and put a hand on her sleeve. "At least you saw her take her first breath. You can sleep at night knowing she's gone to a good family."

She pivoted and placed a palm on his lapel. "How do you know?"

"My grandfather said Old Reverend Playfair handled things. He knows everyone's character, and wouldn't make arrangements to anyone unworthy."

She squinted at him as her voice broke into snivels. "I forgot how small Clanville is."

Yes, it was small, small enough to hide Amora's disappearance. No one, not his Grandfather or Reverend Playfair told him. At the war's end, how would he have handled the news after riding for days to marry a woman who didn't wait for his love?

Chapter Eight: Public Wife

Siphoning a deep breath, Amora entered the Dowager's glittering ball. The crystals of the chandelier danced and sparkled in time with the music. Her pulse slowed as she stared at the myriad of candles. The brightness gave her energy. Mrs. Gretling was right to convince her to attend. She should be here and show Barrington he could depend on her.

A pianoforte tinkled and followed the whipping of violins. Was it Bach? Whatever the tune, it made the carmine red walls seem so lively.

Blinking, she turned and started to look for her husband. A giggling couple missed her toes with inches to spare. Starched cravats and satins the colors of a Hampshire sky twirled around her.

She stopped twiddling her fingers and took six steps forward, but the press of people formed a barrier. Unable to navigate or even see over the thick crowd, Amora settled near the refreshment table. Perhaps when the set cleared, she could see Barrington's powerful form.

The music disappeared. Couples left the half-chalked

floor.

Her stomach lurched when Mr. Charleton sauntered near. With no menacing husband to keep him away, she'd have to talk with him.

"Now, this is a sight to behold." He neared and bowed. "The lovely Amora Tomàs, alone."

"It's Norton, been so for almost five years." She craned her neck, even more so than with Barrington. It was impossible to look around the blonde mountain.

"That's a shame. How could I let him steal you away, Mrs. N-o-r-ton?" He ground out the word with his teeth clenched. His gaze, large with coal black eyes, roamed her face and perhaps, the bugle beads edging her neckline.

The colorless gown might be a blessing tonight.

"To deprive Clanville, all of Hampshire for that matter, of the most magical pianist and painter. It's tortured my soul."

"Barrington Norton never has...tortured a thing." Her breath hitched. Only pure evil attempted such. Hackles rising, she whipped her fan, but the humid air brought no relief. "Sir, I am in no mood for teasing."

"Forgive my clumsy speech. Let me make amends and show you Mother's flowers. I remember how you so loved nature, and the garden should not be missed."

With a shake of her head, she set down her empty cup. "I am looking for my husband. Have you seen Mr. Norton?"

He ran a hand through his golden hair. An unreadable expression dimmed his countenance. "We need to chat. Forget about Norton, the dutiful son Mother wishes she had."

"Sir, don't trifle with me. I must find my husband."

"Your voice is a little loud. Someone might get the wrong impression." He fingered a large gold button on his waistcoat, the Charleton family crest engraved upon it shined in the light. "Fine. I'll help you look."

His insistence and hovering made her count the candle stands. The rumors always linked her to him. It was dangerous to be talking with him. Barrington might see and get the wrong idea. "No, that won't be necessary."

"Two can make better work of any task. I insist." He held out his arm.

Cornered, she took it. Cutting him direct, when the man was only showing kindness, would cause a scene. That would anger Barrington more than entertaining the handsome man.

Mr. Charleton craned his head with enthusiasm and steered her near the balcony.

If he thought her foolish enough to go out on a dark balcony with him, the man was mad. She took her hand away and pivoted. "You haven't changed your flirtatious ways. That's why people accuse you of bad things."

He shrugged. "No moonlight for us? Then I'll check the balcony for you." Pulling back the curtains, he peered through the glass. "Well, well."

She leaned near the opening, but he closed it with great speed, as if the fabric burnt.

"Nothing here, Mrs. Norton. Why don't we return to the refreshment table?"

She squinted at him. The overhead sconce reflected a halo above his light locks.

"What are you hiding, sir?"

His finger settled on the edge of her shimmerless glove. "Nothing a wife should see."

Leveling her shoulders, she pushed past him.

The man moved all too easily out of the way. He wanted her to see. What devilment was he up to?

She split the gold flocked drapes and stared through the glass.

Barrington hugged Cynthia in the moonlight.

Amora couldn't breathe. The curtain fell from her fingers.

"Close your mouth, dear." Charleton's voice stung her ear. "Someone will think something's wrong."

One, two, eight beads on her cuff. Fifteen paces from here to the negus on the table. Two. Two nights of smelling like chrysanthemums.

No crying. No crying. Not in public. Is this why Barrington didn't want her to come? So he could openly parade a mistress?

Her mother could suppress the tears, bottle up the hurt in public. That was, until Papa died. Maybe this is how out of control the woman felt when her world was gone. The Norton marriage was no more.

For the first time in years, she invited the memories of her mother's sharp voice, echoing decorum. "I must find my carriage. Will you escort me in the dark? My abigail's waiting."

"I think you need some punch or let's take a walk in Mother's garden. We can pretend it's summer in Clanville, and you've just painted my portrait."

How could Barrington do this? She peered at her trembling hands. "I've never painted you."

"If we are going to pretend, let's do it big." He nudged her with his elbow.

Men were the devil's handiwork, that and big bosomed singers. "If you're not going to escort me, I'll go alone."

"No, I'll take you. What's a gentleman for if not to be of service?" He led her through the thick crowd.

Disheartened, anger thickening her throat, she held onto his arm. She needed to think. Where could she go to be away from Barrington and everything else she'd lost? Right now disappearing from London, from all of England held an appeal.

"Just a few more steps. Miss Tomàs, remember when your mother sent us to gather apples?"

She wasn't going to correct him this time. Maybe it should still be Tomàs. If she'd told Barrington of the abduction instead of pretending nothing was wrong, he would've abandoned her then. Now, they continually hurt each other. She blinked her eyes, willing away the steam of anger threatening to explode.

They took two more turns and plodded out into a magical garden. Lavender scented the air. Everywhere blooms of yellow, purple, and white with hints of crimson waved in the gentle breeze.

She bristled and let go of his arm. "This isn't the way to my carriage."

He stepped between her and the house, blocking her retreat. "Dear, it's not every day you come face to face with a mistress. You don't have to pretend you're fine."

"From what I recall, you claim those women daily, hourly perhaps." She reached for a flower and counted the delicate petals. "Take me back to the house."

"This is the first time in years I've had a chance to talk with you. Your mother shipped you off to Bath and you took no visitors when you returned."

"I was in no mood to discuss the past then, nor do I wish to now." Heart-pounding, she trudged around him toward the orangery door.

He clasped her arm, stopping her exodus. "I needed to know you were fine."

She shook free. "What? You weren't amused by the rumors of my disappearance."

His eyes grew small. He looked toward the house. "We both know you didn't voluntarily disappear."

She couldn't look at his face anymore. The drumming of her heart eclipsed everything. "I need to go."

"If I'd known you were abducted, I would've looked for you. You're too good of a woman to suffer."

The man had been a favorite family friend. That's why everyone assumed she'd ran away with him. But she didn't. Never would she betray Barrington, even if he'd strayed.

"You in there, Miss Tomàs?" He cupped her chin, raising her head.

Her eyes opened wide as Barrington rammed her friend. He grasped Charleton's chest, hauling him off his feet.

The man broke free. The two exchanged blows.

"I warned you." Barrington made a quick side-step and lunged at the man, wrapping his fingers about Charleton's throat. "You laid hands on my wife."

Charleton sputtered for air. "Stop." He jerked away from Barrington. "Too public a place for murder. And you wouldn't dare, mulatto man, not to my pure blood."

"It was you who hurt her." Barrington seemed possessed. He pounded the stuffing from Charleton's middle and punched him in his fat mouth. "Then you turned on her, for her blood is mixed too. Not good enough to marry, just molest."

What? He'd kill the rake, for what, talking to Amora?

She pulled on her husband's coat. "Let him go. He didn't harm me."

"No, I suppose he didn't. You're old friends." He dropped Charleton's lapel and shoved him to the ground. "Never touch or look at my wife again. She's fragile and easily duped by your false charm."

How? Barrington thought Mr. Charleton tried to charm her. Why did he care after spending the ball in Cynthia's clutches?

Cold gray eyes stared at her, but he couldn't possibly be hurt, not after keeping her at home to continue to his affair.

Charleton patted his split lip with a handkerchief. "Well done, old man. Didn't think you'd do it. Unlike Miss Tomàs, you're so conscious of stupid things. And I'd have married her if she'd consented. We can still wed and be fugitives in Scotland, Amora, my love."

She shook her at the foolishness spewing from both of them. "You're misguided, Mr. Charleton. You too, Mr. Norton."

A light in the third floor of the house brightened as a window flew open. A shadow looked down upon them.

Great. Someone else would see this humiliation. A barrister, a rake and a fragile wife. Right now, she didn't feel fragile. Trapped in the two men's rivalry forced needed heat through her veins. Egyptian pride and honor replaced the hurt of her broken marriage. "Goodnight, gentlemen. You can continue this without me."

"Amora, wait." Barrington reached for her, but she slipped away. She had had enough of smelling chrysanthemums.

Charleton leapt from the ground and dusted his

waistcoat. His shiny gold buttons clanged. "Nothing happened, you Neanderthal."

Barrington raised his fists then lowered it turning to her. "Amora, I asked you to stay."

"I'll escort you to your carriage." Charleton shoved Barrington and came to her side.

Barrington charged toward them. "I told you, not to ___"

Charleton's fist grazed Barrington's jaw, knocking him a few inches. The second strike hit like lightning dropping the mighty oak of a man into the hedges. "Bad form, Norton, deciding you now want your wife after flaunting your mistress. Mind whose company you keep. Go back to the singer."

A wince crossed Barrington's bruised cheek as he attempted to stand. "Charleton, we will settle this score later. Amora, stop."

"Mr. Charleton, Mr. Norton, enjoy the rest of the party. I'm sure you both can find other entertainment. Or go beat one another senseless. I'll have a footman escort me."

Lifting her head, she followed the lighted path back into the house. No more fighting for this marriage or her sanity, neither was worth the trouble.

It took an hour and a half for James to get the carriage out of the traffic. Being early to the ball didn't bode well for trying to leave and chase after his wife.

She came. Why?

The side of Barrington's face throbbed from the bone beneath his eye to his jaw. Charleton looked well pleased, taunting him. And he threw a vicious punch like old times. What would be the ramifications for darkening the rake's daylights?

He couldn't think about that, just Amora and Charleton. Blast it. Cynthia's gossip had to be true. Charleton must be the man who seduced Amora. But if that was so, why wasn't she terrified of him now? Would the end of their relationship cause nightmares? None of this made sense. Tonight, he'd get answers.

Arriving at Mayfair, James opened the carriage door. "A gentle, steady hand catches more fish than one raging."

Barrington stared into his dark eyes. "Not this time."

The sky was light. The sun would be out soon. It was time for the truth to rise as well. He pounded into the townhome and charged the steps. Turning the knob of her chamber, he found it locked.

He moved his palm above the threshold and found the housekeeper's screw resting on the upper trim. Unlocking it, he tossed the door open. The room felt cold. No fire in her mantle and the window lay open, allowing a breeze. He stepped inside and stopped. His mouth dropped open.

Amora wasn't at her vanity or in bed. She lay asleep on the floor, all balled up as if that would hide her. Her fingers curled around a heavy Dresden figurine of a rhinoceros.

His heart crushed a little more. Did she think he'd hit her? Didn't she know him?

He'd never been violent with her. He'd prosecuted men for harming women. A little unsteady, he used all of his energy to scoop her up and carried her to the bed. She opened one eye, then wrapped her arms about his neck. "You've come to save me."

Sucking in a breath, he set her onto the mattress. Hip

pulsing with pain, he dropped beside her. "I've come for answers. Why did you come to the Dowager's? You were to stay home."

Her lips curled to a frown as her eyes darted left and right. "I thought I could show you I could be supportive. I don't want to be fragile."

Her fingers scalloped the bruises on his cheek. The delicate touch tortured and tingled. "But only rumors will fly now."

He couldn't think of that. He closed his eyes. "Did you run off with Charleton while I was at war?"

"No."

"Admit you ran off with someone." He tugged at his wilted cravat and tried to be calm. He failed miserably.

"I did not."

"Amora, you went willingly. It was a seduction, but you made up the story so your mother wouldn't be judgmental."

"No, but she didn't believe me either. Not at first." She answered in clear, strong tones. "No one did."

He couldn't accept her answer, not after witnessing Charleton about to kiss her. "Just say the words. I need to hear the truth."

She pulled away and swept a blanket onto her legs. "Is that the excuse you need to justify taking a mistress?"

"Nonsense. You're trying to distract from my line of questioning." He was the one deceived, not her. Bounding up, he scooped up a chair and pulled it near. He sank into it adjusting his weight, taking pressure off his hip. Not ready to ease up on the witness, he lowered his voice and took a new tact. "Tell me what made Mrs. Tomàs believe your story?"

She opened her mouth then closed it. "Does it matter? You've already convicted me. Please leave."

"My wife, the woman whom I believed loved me and waited faithfully for my return, just gave up. An innocent person fights, yells out."

"A tired person waits for things to end." Her tone sounded flat, not the vigor of the woman who'd stomped away from Charleton and him.

"Then we need to go ask Mrs. Tomàs." He stood and hobbled to the door. "Get dressed. We go to Clanville within the hour."

He'd know everything by the day's end. Then he'd figure out how to fix what remained of his marriage.

Get the next Episode in February 2016. Join my newsletter to stay informed and if you liked this please leave a review.

Sneak Peak: Episode II

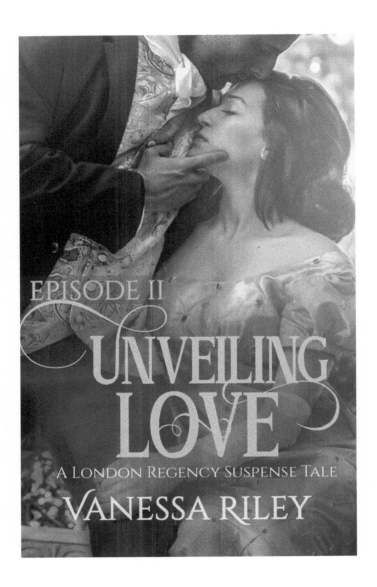

EPISODE II

UNVEILING
LOVE

A LONDON REGENCY SUSPENSE TALE

VANESSA RILEY

Episode II of Unveiling Love
Length: 8 Chapters (28,000 words)
Summary: The Ungodly Truth

Barrington Norton has always despised lies and has formed his life upon a foundation of truth. Yet, discovering the truth of Amora's past sends him to the breaking point. How can he ever make amends for not believing her? Will she ever love him as she once did?

Amora Norton is tired, tired of fighting for her marriage and her sanity. Now that she understands how fleeting Barrington's love is, she wants none of it. It may be better off being alone than living with pity. Having lost all, can she find herself?

Nonetheless, a serial abductor is at large, awakening to existence of the one that got away. Only a united couple can put an end to his reign of terror.

Pre-order/order the next <u>Episode</u> which releases February 2016. Join my <u>newsletter</u> to stay informed and if you liked this please leave a review.

Here's your sneak peak at the next episode.

Chapter One: London, March 1, 1819

Rain splashed against the glass of the carriage as it rumbled down the road. Amora sat on her hands across from Barrington. Barely a word exchanged between them since their harrowing flight from London at dawn.

He'd caught her asleep on the floor, but his anger at the fight at his patroness's home must've made him forget. Good. He'd have a lot more to understand once they arrived at Tomàs Manor.

In another hour or so, Mother would give him answers he'd never expect. Sleeping on the floor wouldn't seem so bad, but would Barrington understand? Could a man ever fully understand being made a victim, knowing other victims? Could he ever accept be so low and helpless? Never. Not Barrington.

She glanced at him again. His bruised countenance bobbled as his head zigged and zagged along the seatback. His snow-white cravat fluttered with each short snore.

He hadn't shaved. Not how he liked to start his day with light stubble edging his chin. At least he'd changed his clothes from his soiled evening pantaloons and coat.

Oh, that horrid party. His reputation must be in tatters. What would be the repercussions for a mulatto, a black, striking a member of the ton?

A sigh left her like a billow used to stoke flames, only she had none. Her fire was gone. He didn't believe her. The man she loved thought her wanton, just like mother.

And how could she forgive him constantly being with Cynthia? How strong of man could he be with a tart constantly trying to give him pie? Even a self-righteous man could get hungry.

She pushed at her brow, trying to remember what happiness was. It wasn't in the carriage, or London. Certainly not with Mother. Yet, did happiness exist with Barrington, being with him, being married to him? She count the days on one pinky, the moments she didn't fret over his opinions, his wants, his desires.

With her middles stewing, she balled her fists, hiding the unnumbered fingers. When he discovered how wrong he was to believe Cynthia's lies, could Amora ever fully trust that he'd never have another moment in which doubts about her honor would win?

With a shake of her head, she turned to the window and the endless streams of water. Surely, that must be a bad omen. Yes, his god was still angry with her. Maybe mother's Isis, too.

"Gerald, no!" Barrington bolted up. His grey eyes were vacant, then beset with heavy blinks. He rubbed his face and peered out the window. "We are getting close. Pity to visit Mrs. Tomàs on such a wet day."

"Weeks away from yuletide, she'll probably be too busy with things. She'll not care, and she's used to me showing up looking like a drowned rat. If she tries to get us to stay, don't agree."

His lips thinned as he tugged at his lapel. "Rat? What does that mean and explain last night, too? Why did you come to the ball? And why were you alone with, Charleton?"

"That's a lot of questions. A famed Barrington Norton interrogation." She folded her arms about her cape. "Why don't you explain yourself? Why did you not want me to go, and why were you embracing Cynthia Miller? No, I forgot. The accused can't ask questions."

He leaned back as his frown lifted in a smirk. "Clever. Madam judge can ask questions of a barrister. I have nothing to hide. I do apologize for causing a scene. Simply lost my head when I saw you with a rake."

"No other explanations?" She tilted her head forward. Her heavy heart made her wobble a bit. "You touched a peer, an innocent one. The ramifications--"

"I'll deal with that. My short absence might be warranted, but I doubt Charleton will do anything of it, for it will expose him too and you. He's so fond of you."

She held inside her irritation at his lack of belief in her. "Well, Cynthia Miller will miss you. And don't deny it. I saw you two."

"What?" He rubbed his jaw. "So that's how Charleton tricked you, with jealousy. She's very emotional right now. Caught in some trouble, but my investigator will solve that."

Amora tried hard not to roll her eyes but the hope that she'd see something other than ridicule or stupidity on her insides was too great. "Always helping others. That jade won't bother Beakes. She finds reasons to be around you. Can't you see she's in love with you? That she'll use anything to twist you up, to compromise you?"

"Preposterous. She's Gerald Miller's little sister. I need to protect her. Miller saved my life. I owe it to him."

Barrington leaned forward. His smirk increased. "So out of jealousy, you went alone with a rake to the garden. Convenient of him being able to give you a tour."

"I thought... " She turned her head and tried to search for the right words to convince him, but the old spire of the priory came into view. A chill raced through her down to the boning of her corset. Images of it, the last thing she'd painted before her abduction plagued her mind. That horrible day - grabbed out of her slippers, beating on masculine arms that had to have been forged in iron - stuck in her head. One. Two. Hard to breathe.

Something caught her hand.

She jerked away, but only witnessed Barrington's concerned pout. He'd joined her on her seat. "We could go straight to Cornwall. A couple of notes at the next post off to Hessing, and we could start anew."

He put an arm about her back, toyed with a raven curl poking from her bonnet. "You just have a price to pay." Pulling closer to her ear, his whispered breaths kissed her lobe. "Just the truth, Amora."

How dare he?

How could he try to seduce her into a lie, because he couldn't accept the truth? She stiffened, tried to push away, but he crowded her. How ironic. She usually crowded him.

"Please, Amora."

His sweet strong voice made her want to curl up in his lap and retreat into the safety of his arms like last night. But, could she pay the price? She didn't have any more lies to give, just ugly truths.

She said no with a shake of her head and shoved on

his chest. "Go back to your seat, Barr."

His grey eyes smoldered. He lifted her palm and put his lips to them. "Don't you want to start anew? Pay the piper. Own your lies, all of them."

Pulse rising, pounding in despair, she wrenched away. Hurt at his words and her terrible weakness for him. "Stop it. I'm not in the mood to be bedded and then dismissed again."

Barrington blinked and sat back. "Amora, I am ready to hear your side. I'll forgive anything. I just need the truth."

"Go to your seat. Take your suspicions with you."

Hands in the air, he lunged to his side of the carriage. "I'm trying to make this easier for you. There's vanity in falsehoods. It's best to own our mistakes."

"My own flesh and blood, the woman who birthed me didn't believe me. Why should the man I wed?"

She looked to her lap and folded her hands beneath the creamy wool of her stole. Only a stranger, Vicar Wilson, and perhaps, Mr. Charleton understood. She slumped against the window and counted tufts of white silk lining the carriage walls. "Mother will tell you what you want to know."

Until this moment, she didn't realize how similar her Mama and Barrington were. No wonder neither loved her enough.

Gunshots rang out.

Barrington's gaze shot to the carriage window. The rain had stopped but low clouds still filled the sky. Traveling on the back roads held a certain amount of danger, but he always rode prepared.

He ran a finger along the knob fastening the

compartment under the seat. James kept a gun oiled inside and stocked with plenty of bullet packets. He'd protect his wife from bandits. No one would ever have a chance to hurt her again. No rake or bandit.

Another gun belched. The sound was a high pitch squeal. That was a small weapon, one not built for war or highwaymen. He eased back onto his seat.

Amora rubbed her temples. "Mother must be practicing her pistols. She hasn't done that since Papa... in a long time."

As the carriage came to a stop, he spied Mrs. Tomàs traipsing from the orchards toward the large house. Her raven hair bounced with each step. The simple straw bonnet did a poor job of keeping her tresses orderly.

Coming from the direction of the big stable house, the unusual woman, with skin almost as dark as his, carried a flintlock and dangled it by her side. So unlike the fastidious lady of his memories, the one who belittled his stature, his race, his personal small fortune absent his grandfather's wealth, even his father's waywardness on their last meeting. For Amora, Henutsen Tomàs had wanted a man of noble blood like the Charletons or truthfully any white gentleman of means.

The heat in his lungs started to burn his nostrils. He extended his arm to Amora. "Last chance."

Chin high, she pushed past him and plodded up the steps to the wide portico. "Let's be done with this."

His feet became weighty lead. He held onto the door of the carriage. His plan to learn the truth no longer seemed like a good one. How much worse would he feel when Mrs. Tomàs confirmed his suspicions?

Or even worse.

What if she didn't and Amora was truly abducted,

how would he make up for his lack of trust?

Thunder clapped. He tensed adding pressure to the bullet wound in his hip. A just reward for acting like a jealous fool and riding hours in a carriage. Shaking out his leg, he eased to the ground. "James, refresh the horses in the stables. This could take awhile."

His man nodded and moved the carriage forward. Barrington hurried and caught up to his wife.

"Mr. Norton, Amora? What are you doing here?" His mother-in-law set her gun down and wiped her hands on the sides of her dark colored walking dress. "I would have prepared something had I known."

Barrington step forward and bowed his head. "We've come to ask you questions."

"He came to ask questions." Amora moved behind him almost as if she hid.

What could she be afraid of? Mrs. Tomàs wasn't much taller than she. They shared similar body weights, nothing to fear.

"Mr. Norton, looks like you caught the bad end of a fight. But you look well, dear." The older woman swiped at her face and held her arms open, beckoning with nods for Amora to come.

Her daughter bristled and stepped away. She slunk to the corner and clung to one of the whitewashed posts supporting the covered roof. "Tell Barrington what happened."

Her voice sounded short, hot like fire. Then it died away in the increasing wind. She played with the buttons on her cream redingote. Three people stood on the portico. How could it be possible for her to seem so alone?

Mrs. Tomàs retrieved her shawl from a chair sitting

against the wall. I've missed you, sweetheart. Let me get the cook to make you something to eat."

Undoing the strings of her egret feather bonnet, Amora kept her focus toward the thick grove of trees, the start of the Tomàs Orchards. "Get the papers. It's time to show him."

Tears dribbled down his mother-in-law's stoic face as she moved near her daughter and stroked her back. "Are you sure?"

"Yes. Barrington, follow her." The tone smoldered again, short, punctuated, determined. "Ask your questions. Find your truth."

He adjusted his spectacles. Part of him wanted to embrace his wife and tell her he'd changed his mind, but that wouldn't stop his questions. No, only the truth would.

He took note of her stiff posture, her expressionless gaze toward the trees. She didn't seem like one fearing exposure, but she didn't cry out her innocence either.

The Old Bailey would convict her.

Hadn't he?

Order the next Episode.

Extras

Author's Note

Dear Friend,

I enjoyed writing Unveiled Love because diverse Regency London needs its story told, and I am a sucker for a wonderful husband and wife romance. They need love after the vows, too.

These stories will showcase a world of intrigue and romance, a setting everyone can hopefully find a character to identify with in the battle of love, which renews and gives life.

Stay in touch. Sign up at www.vanessariley.com for my newsletter. You'll be the first to know about upcoming releases, and maybe even win a sneak peek.

Thank so much for giving this book a read.

Vanessa Riley

Many of my readers are new to Regencies, so I always add notes and a glossary to make items readily available. If you know of a term that should be added to enhance my readers' knowledge, send them to me at: vanessa@christianregency.com. I will acknowledge you in my next book.

Here are my notes:

Mulatto Barristers

I couldn't find definitive proof of one, but that does not mean it was impossible. Connections and success bent rules. Such was the case for William Garrow (1760-1840). He was not born a gentleman and didn't go to the best schools. Yet, his success in the courts rewrote how trials would be performed. He introduced the premise, "presumed innocent until proven guilty," and rose to become Solicitor General for England and Wales.

Free blacks in 1800's English Society

By Regency times, historians, Kirstin Olsen and Gretchen Holbrook Gerzina, estimate that Black London (the black neighborhood of London) had over 10,000 residents. While England led the world in granting rights to the enslaved and ending legal slavery thirty years before the American Civil War, it still had many citizens who were against change. Here is another image from an anti-abolitionist.

The New Union Club Being a Representation of what took place at a celebrated Dinner given by a celebrated society – includes in picture abolitionists, Billy Waters, Zachariah Macauley, William Wilberforce. – published

19 July 1819. Source: Wiki Commons

Inter-racial marriages occurred.

The children known as mulattos lived lives on the scale of their education and wealth. Examine this painting. Portrait of a Mulatto by FABRE, François-Xavier. It is from 1809-1810. Portraits were indicative to status and wealth. My screenshot of the image the art once displayed at Arenski Fine Art, LTD London. More information can be found at http:// maryrobinettekowal.com/journal/images-of-regency-era-free-people-of-colour/.

This painting of an interracial couple and child, *Pintura de Castas*, from Spaniard and Mulatto, Morisca (1763). Where love exists barriers fade.

Slavery in England

The emancipation of slaves in England preceded America by thirty years and freedom was won by legal court cases not bullets.

Somerset v Stewart (1772) is a famous case, which established the precedence for the rights of slaves in England. The English Court of King's Bench, led by Lord Mansfield, decided that slavery was unsupported by the common law of England and Wales. His ruling:

"The state of slavery is of such a nature that it is incapable of being introduced on any reasons, moral or political, but only by positive law, which preserves its force long after the reasons, occasions, and time itself from whence it was created, is erased from memory. It is so odious, that nothing can be suffered to support it, but positive law. Whatever inconveniences, therefore, may follow from the decision, I cannot say this case is allowed or approved by the law of England; and therefore the black must be discharged."

E. Neville William, The Eighteenth-Century Constitution: 1688-1815, pp: 387-388.

The Slavery Abolition Act 1833 was an act of Parliament, which abolished slavery throughout the British Empire. A fund of $20 Million Pound Sterling was set up to compensate slave owners. Many of the highest society families were compensated for losing their slaves.

This act did exempt the territories in the possession of the East India Company, the Island of Ceylon, and the Island of Saint Helena. In 1843, the exceptions were eliminated.

Glossary

The Regency – The Regency is a period of history from 1811-1825 (sometimes expanded to 1795-1837) in England. It takes its name from the Prince Regent who ruled in his father's stead when the king suffered mental illness. The Regency is known for manners, architecture, and elegance. Jane Austen wrote her famous novel, *Pride and Prejudice* (1813), about characters living during the Regency.

England is a country in Europe. London is the capital city of England.

Image of England from a copper engraved map created by William Darton in 1810.

Port Elizabeth was a town founded in 1820 at the tip of South Africa. The British settlement was an attempt to strengthen England's hold on the Cape Colony and to be a buffer from the Xhosa.

Xhosa - A proud warrior people driven to defend their land and cattle-herding way of life from settlers expanding the boundaries of the Cape Colony.

Image of South Africa from a copper engraved map created by John Dower in 1835.

Abigail – A lady's maid.

Soiree – An evening party.

Bacon-brained – A term meaning foolish or stupid.

Black – A description of a black person or an African.

Black Harriot – A famous prostitute stolen from Africa, then brought to England by a Jamaican planter who died, leaving her without means. She turned to harlotry to earn a living. Many members of the House of Lords became her clients. She is described as tall, genteel, and alluring, with a degree of politeness.

Blackamoor – A dark-skinned person.

Bombazine – Fabric of twilled or corded cloth made of silk and wool or cotton and wool. Usually the material was dyed black and used to create mourning clothes.

Breeched – The custom of a young boy no longer wearing pinafores and now donning breeches. This occurs about age six.

Breeches – Short, close-fitting pants for men, which fastened just below the knees and were worn with stockings.

Caning – A beating typically on the buttocks for naughty behavior.

Compromise – To compromise a reputation is to ruin or cast aspersions on someone's character by catching them with the wrong people, being alone with someone who wasn't a relative at night, or being caught doing something wrong. During the Regency, gentlemen were often forced to marry women they had compromised.

Dray – Wagon.

Footpads – Thieves or muggers in the streets of London.

Greatcoat – A big outdoor overcoat for men.

Mews – A row of stables in London for keeping horses.

Pelisse - An outdoor coat for women that is worn over a dress.

Quizzing Glass – An optical device, similar to a monocle, typically worn on a chain. The wearer might use the quizzing glass to look down upon people.

Reticule – A cloth purse made like a bag that had a drawstring closure.

Season – One of the largest social periods for high society in London. During this time, a lady attended a variety of balls and soirees to meet potential mates.

Sideboard – A low piece of furniture the height of a writing desk, which housed spirits.

Ton – Pronounced *tone*, the *ton* was a high class in society during the Regency era.

Sneak Peak: Unmasked Heart

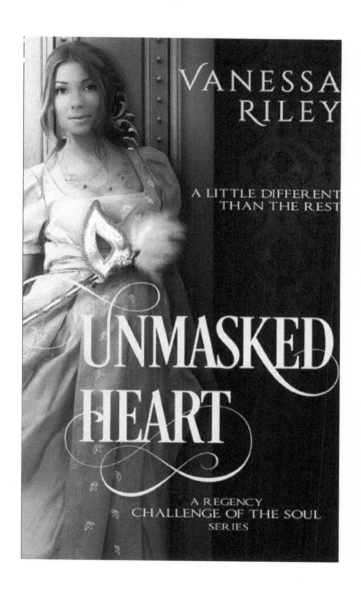

VANESSA
RILEY

A LITTLE DIFFERENT
THAN THE REST

UNMASKED
HEART

A REGENCY
CHALLENGE OF THE SOUL
SERIES

Shy, nearsighted caregiver, Gaia Telfair always wondered why her father treated her a little differently than her siblings, but she never guessed she couldn't claim his love because of a family secret, her illicit birth. With everything she knows to be true evaporating before her spectacles, can the mulatto passing for white survive being exposed and shunned by the powerful duke who has taken an interest in her?

Ex-warrior, William St. Landon, the Duke of Cheshire, will do anything to protect his mute daughter from his late wife's scandals. With a blackmailer at large, hiding in a small village near the cliffs of Devonshire seems the best option, particularly since he can gain help from the talented Miss Telfair, who has the ability to help children learn to speak. If only he could do a better job at shielding his heart from the young lady, whose honest hazel eyes see through his jests as her tender lips challenge his desire to remain a single man.

Unmasked Heart is the first Challenge of the Soul Regency novel.

Excerpt from Unmasked Heart: The Wrong Kiss

Seren adjusted the delicate gauzy silk flowers lining the edges of Gaia's cape. "Wait here until your Elliot arrives. Don't leave this room; I'll come back to find you."

Part of Gaia didn't want to release Seren's hand. Half-seeing things made the room frightening. Her pulse raced. "What if someone else arrives?"

"Tell them the room is occupied. They'll understand." Seren adjusted her silvery sarsenet cape, balanced the scales she hung on a cord in place of a reticule, and smoothed her wide skirts.

Grasping hold of the armrest, Gaia forced her lips to smile. "Good luck to you, Lady Justice. I hope you have fun."

"If you find the love you seek, I'll be happy. You deserve happiness for being you, not someone's daughter. Tell Elliot of your love. Gaia, you need a name and a household of your own, where secrets can't harm you." She gave Gaia a hug. "I want your cup filled with joy."

"Even if my cup isn't pure."

"Your heart is untainted by the past, made pure by salvation. That's what matters." Seren put a hand to Gaia's face. In the candlelight, she and Seren, their skin, looked the same. "Live free tonight."

Seren moved out of focus and left the room, closing the door behind her.

The lime blur of the settee was as comfortable as it was big, but Gaia couldn't sit still. She fidgeted and tapped her slippers on the floor. The ticking of the mantle clock filled the quiet room.

Trying to ignore it, she clutched the ribbons of her papier-mâché mask and straightened its creamy feathers. She stood and, with the pace of a turtle, she moved to the fireplace and strained to see where the limbs of timepiece pointed. Nine-fifteen.

Elliot would be here soon. What would she say to him? Would she remain silent and just dance with him?

She leveled her shoulders. How could she not say her peace, as she looked into his blue eyes? How ironic to unmask her heart at a masquerade ball.

The moon finally broke through the clouds and cast its light into the salon. Whether from the fuzziness of her vision or the beauty of the glow, the window glass sparkled, as did the mirrors and polished candleholders of the small room.

The low tones of the musicians started up again. The jaunty steps of a reel sounded. The tone called to her feet again, and she danced as if she were in someone's arms. The beechnut- colored walls and white moldings swirled as she did.

That set ended and then another and another. She paced in front of the mantle clock. It tolled a low moan as it struck ten. Elliot had missed their appointment. Heaviness weighed upon Gaia, from the crown of her costume's veils to the thick folds of her opal domino.

How ironic to stand in such finery, when Mr. Telfair told her she wasn't worthy. Yet hadn't she schemed with her stepmother and Seren to be here? Gaia should leave. Too many wrongs would never equal righteousness.

Movement outside the room sent her pulse racing. Maybe Elliot had been detained, but was still coming. She wrung her hands and looked to the shining circle on the door, its crystal knob.

The footsteps passed by, the sound diminishing, as did her dreams.

Elliot wouldn't show. He must still think of her as a child, as Julia's hapless sister, as Millicent's plain cousin. Or maybe Julia had told him. They could be laughing about it now.

Sighs and a misguided tear leaked out. She leaned against the burnished mantle. The warmth of the hearth did nothing to thaw her suddenly-cold feet. It was best he didn't show. He'd saved her the embarrassment of his rejection. A mulatto's dance or kiss could never do for him.

The rhythm of a dance set crept beneath the ivory doorframe. Maybe Elliot found a new young lady, whose large dowry like Millicent's made her irresistible to men. Was she in his arms, basking in the glow of his smile, his fun conversation?

The ache in her bosom swelled. Gaia released her breath, stilling her trembling fingers against the sheer veil of her fairy costume. Perhaps she should slip from the room and run into the moonlight of the moors.

The door opened. The strains of violin-play seeped into the salon.

Elliot in his domino cape and ebony half-mask entered the room. "Excuse me," his voice was low, hoarse. He whipped a handkerchief from his pocket and wiped his mouth as he bowed.

Always so formal, but what a pity his melodious voice sounded raspy.

Now or never. She cleared her throat and, in her most sultry manner, she placed her hands to her hips and curtsied. "I've been waiting for you."

"Excuse me, do I know you?" He tugged at the ribbons of his mask.

Waving her arms, she caught his gaze. "Please don't take it off. I won't be able to get through this if you expose your handsome face."

"I see." He stopped, his strong hands lowering beneath the cape of his domino. "Miss Telfair?"

With a quick motion, she whipped up her airy silk skirts and traipsed closer, but maintained an easy distance on the other side of the settee. "Call me Gaia.

We needn't be so formal."

His head moved from side-to-side, as if to scan the room.

"You needn't fret, sir. We are quite alone. That's why I decided to confess my feelings."

"I see."

Must he continue to act as if he didn't know her? The moonbeams streaming through the thick window mullions surrounded him, and reflected in the shiny black silk of his cape. Could he be taller, more intimidating?

Elliot had to think of her as a woman. She straightened her shoulders. "I'm so glad you've come. I know I'm young, but not too young to know my heart."

"Miss Telfair, I think this is some sort of mistake."

Blood pounding in her ears, she swept past the settee and stood within six feet of him. "Please call me Gaia."

"I'll not trespass on your privacy any longer." He spun, as if to flee.

She shortened the distance and caught his shoulder. "Please don't go. It took a lot to garner the courage to meet you here."

With a hesitance she'd never seen from confident Elliot, he gripped her palm and kissed her satin glove. "I know it takes a great amount of courage to make a fool of one's self."

"There's no better fool than one in love." She slipped his hand to her cheek. "Why hide behind mocking? I know you. I've seen your heart. The way you take care of that precious little girl as if she were your own." It touched Gaia, witnessing Elliot helping his brother's household as if it were his own.

"How did you know my fear?" He drew his hand to

his mouth. "You see too much."

Squinting, he still wasn't quite in focus. He shifted his weight and rubbed his neck, as if her compliments made him nervous.

"This is a mistake. We should forget this conversation. A man shouldn't be alone with such a forthright young lady. I will return to the ball." He leveled his broad shoulders and marched to the door, his heels clicking the short distance.

Maybe being so low was freeing. "Why leave?" she let her voice sound clear, no longer cautioned with shyness or regret. "Here can be no worse than out there, with the other ladies readying to weigh your pockets."

His feet didn't move, but he closed the door, slamming it hard. Had she struck a nerve?

He pivoted to face her. "Aren't you just like them, my dear? Weren't all gentle women instructed to follow a man's purse? No? Perhaps torturing is your suit, demanding more and more until nothing remains of his soul."

"Men hunt for dowries, and they know best how to torture someone; ignoring people who want their best; separating friends, even sisters, in their pursuits. The man who raised me did so begrudgingly, just to make me a governess to my brother. Is there no worse torture than to yearn to be loved and no one care?"

"A governess? I think I understand."

This wasn't how she'd expected this conversation to go. Elliot's graveled words possessed an edge as sharp as a sword. He seemed different, both strong and vulnerable. It must be the costumes, freeing them both from the confining roles they lived.

Yet he didn't move. He didn't feel the same.

She fanned her shimmering veil. Half-seeing and disguised, she could be as bold and as direct as Millicent or Seren. Gaia could even face the truth. "I forgive you for not feeling the same."

She'd said it, and didn't crumble when he didn't respond in kind. Maybe this was best. With the release of a pent-up breath, she added, "I wish you well."

He chuckled, the notes sounding odd for Elliot's laugh. "Has a prayer wrought this transformation? Well, He works in mysterious ways."

Maybe it was all the prayers over the years that built up her strength. Amazing. Elliot didn't love her, and no tears came to her. Well, numbness had its benefit. "Good evening. You can go; my friend Seren will be back soon."

When he finally moved, it was to come closer, near enough she trail her pinkie along the edgings of his domino, but that, too, was a cliff she wasn't ready to jump.

"Gaia, what if I'm not ready to leave?"

Her ears warmed, throbbing with the possibilities of his meaning.

"If I am trapped," his voice dropped to a whisper, "it is by your hands."

Her heart clenched at his words. Elliot never seemed more powerful or more dangerous. "I'd hope I, ah, maybe I should be leaving."

He took a half-step, as if to block her path. His outline remained a blur; a tall, powerful blur. "You've had your say, sweet Gaia. Now it is my turn."

This near, she could smell the sweet starch of his thick cravat and a bit of spice. Her heart beat so loudly. Could he hear it?

He drew a thumb down her cheek. "Pretty lady, your

eyes are red. Your cheeks are swollen. What made you cry so hard? And why didn't you find me?"

Something was different about the tone of his hushed voice. There was pain in it. Did he hurt because Gaia had? Could she have discounted the possibility of Elliot returning affections too quickly?

Something dark and formidable drew her to him like never before. "How could I find you? I didn't know you cared, not until this moment."

His arms went about her, and he cradled her against his side. His fingers lighted in her bun. "I'm fascinated with the curl and color of your hair."

Too many thoughts pressed as a familiar tarragon scent tightened its grip about her heart. "Not course or common—"

His lips met her forehead. His hot breath made her shiver and lean more into him. "Never; that's what I've been trying to tell you."

Heady, and a little intoxicated by the feel of his palms on her waist, she released her mask. It fluttered to the floor. Its pole drummed then went silent on the wood floor. She dropped her lids and raised her chin. "I guess this is when you kiss me. Know the lips of someone who esteems you, not your means or connections."

"A lass as beautiful as you needn't ask or wait for a buffoon to find you alone in a library." His arm tightened about her, and he pulled her beneath his cape. The heat of him made her swoon, dipping her head against his broad chest. He tugged a strand of her curls, forcing her chignon to unravel and trail her back. "Now you look the part of a fairy, an all-knowing auburn-haired Gypsy."

He lifted her chin and pressed his mouth against her sealed lips. However, with less than a few seconds of rapture, he relented and released her shoulders.

She wrapped her arms about his neck and wouldn't release him. "I'm horrible. This is my first kiss. I'm sorry." She buried her face against his waistcoat.

His quickened breath warmed her cheek. "Then it should be memorable." His head dipped forward, with the point of his mask, the delicate paper nose, trailing her brows, nudging her face to his. Slowly drawing a finger across her lips, his smooth nail, the feel of his rough warm skin, made them vibrate, relax, then part. "Trust me, Gaia."

She wanted to nod her consent, but didn't dare move from his sensuous touch.

"Let a real kiss come from a man who covets your friendship, who thinks you are beautiful." He dropped his domino to the floor.

Read more of Unmasked Heart at VanessaRiley.com.

Sneak Peak: The Bargain III

Episode III of The Bargain
Length: 11 Chapters (30,000 words)
Summary: Secrets Revealed

Excerpt: The Aftermath of a Kiss and the Xhosa

"Captain," Ralston cleared his throat. "She fixed me up and a number of others."

The baron's lips pursed as he nodded. "Miss Jewell is full of surprises."

His hair was wild and loose. He smelled of beach sand and perspiration. Still frowning, he raised Ralston's arm a few inches from the boat's deck. "Looks like you will live."

"Don't know how much good that'll do me here, Captain. We left here with peace. Why? What happened? And Mr. Narvel?"

"I don't know, but I'm going to find the answers." Using Mr. Ralston's good arm, the captain pulled him to stand. "Get yourself below and sleep. I've got men on watch. Our guns are ready this time for any other surprises."

The sailor shrugged as he tested his shoulder, pushing at the wrapped muscles. "Yes, Sir."

Lord Welling leaned down and took Precious's hand. "You've helped enough, Miss Jewell. I want you to go down below."

She shook her head. "There's more I can do up here."

The baron snatched her up by the elbow. "I insist."

Precious shook free and grabbed up the doctoring supplies. "We're probably going to need these again."

Ralston closed his eyes and grunted almost in unison

with Lord Welling before trudging past the other men laying out on the deck, the one's whose injured legs prevented them from going below. With no rain, they'd be alright under the night sky.

Precious looked up into the night sky that looked like black velvet with twinkling diamonds. Such innocence shrouds this place. So opposite the truth.

"Come along, Miss Jewel. Now." The baron's voice sounded of distant thunder, quiet and potent. His patience, his anger, at so many lost this night must be stirring. He again put his hands around her shoulders and swept her forward.

She didn't like to be turned so abruptly, but stopping in her tracks didn't seem right either. So she slowed her steps, dragging her slippers against the planks of the Margeaux. "What are you doing?"

He stopped and swung her around so that she faced him. "I need your help telling Mrs. Narvel. It's not going to be easy telling a pregnant woman that—"

"Her husband has died at the Xhosa's hands." Precious's heart drummed loudly, like a death gait. Staying busy helping the injured delayed the building grief she had for her friend. Oh, how was Clara to take it?

Lord Welling's lips thinned and pressed into a line. "It's never easy telling a woman a difficult truth or waiting for her to admit it."

She caught his gaze. It felt as if the fire within it scorched her. Suddenly, the smell of him, the closeness of his stance made her pulse race. He wasn't talking about Clara, but Precious wasn't ready to admit anything.

And what would he think if she told him that at that

moment with Xhosa bearing down upon them that nothing seemed more right than to dive headlong to save him. No, Lord Welling didn't need that bug in his ear.

But soon, he'd press. He wasn't the kind of man who waited for anything.

He gripped her hand and led her into the darkness where those stars twinkled in his eyes. "Precious, I need to ask you something."

Chin lifting, she pushed past him and headed for the hole and the ladder below. "We need to get to Mrs. Narvel."

She took her time climbing down, making sure of her footing on each rung, then she waited at the bottom for her employer, the man who in the middle of chaos kissed her more soundly than any one ever had.

His boots made a gentle thud as he jumped the last rungs. When he pivoted, he crowded her in the dark corner, towering over her. "You're reckless, Precious."

She backed up until she pressed against the compartment's planked wall. "I'm not the only one. Taking Jonas to a land of killing, that's reckless."

He clutched the wall above each of her shoulders, but he might as well had gripped them with his big hands. There was no escape from the truth he was waiting on.

Leaning within an inch of her, his voice reached a loud scolding tone. "You're reckless. Wanton for danger."

Her face grew warm and she bit down on her traitorous lips, ones that wanted a taste of him again.

His breathing seemed noisier. His hands moved to within inches of her arms, but they didn't sneak about her. No, those fingers stayed flat against the wood, tempting, teasing of comfort. "You could've been killed. Will you ever listen?"

The harshness of his tone riled up her spirit. "Won't do me no good to listen if you're dead. The least you can say is thank you."

He straightened and towed one hand to his neck. Out of habit, she squinted as if he'd strike her, but she knew in her bones that wasn't to happen. The fear of him hurting her was long gone. Only the fright of him acting again on that kiss between them remained. "What am I to do with you?"

Get the next Episode. Look for all the episodes. Join my newsletter to stay informed.

Join My Newsletter, Free Goodies

If you like this story and want more, please offer a review on Amazon or Goodreads.

Also, sign up for my newsletter and get the latest news on this series or even a free book. I appreciate your support.

VR

Let me point you to some free books, just for reading this far:

Free Book: The Bargain - Episode I:

Coming to London has given Precious Jewell a taste of freedom, and she will do anything, bear anything, to keep it. Defying her master is at the top of her mind, and she won't let his unnerving charm sway her. Yet, will her restored courage lead her to forsake a debt owed to the grave and a child who is as dear to her as her own flesh?

Gareth Conroy, the third Baron Welling, can neither abandon his upcoming duty to lead the fledgling colony of Port Elizabeth, South Africa nor find the strength to be a good father to his heir. Every look at the boy reminds him of the loss of his wife. Guilt over her death plagues his sleep, particularly when he returns to London. Perhaps the spirit and fine eyes of her lady's maid, Precious Jewell, might offer the beleaguered baron a new reason to dream.

Free Book: A Taste of Traditional Regency Romances: Extended excerpts of Regency novels (Bluestocking League Book 1)

From some of the most beloved authors of Regency romance come stories to delight. These excerpts, set in the time of Jane Austen, will give you a sip of sweet romance and will leave you eager for more.

Gail Eastwood, The Captain's Dilemma: Escaped French war prisoner Alexandre Valmont has risked life and honor in a desperate bid to return home and clear his name. Merissa Pritchard risks charges of treason and her family's safety to help the wounded fugitive. But will they risk their hearts in a most dangerous game of love?

From Camille Elliot, The Spinster's Christmas: Spinster Miranda Belmoore and naval Captain Gerard Foremont, old childhood friends, meet again for a large Christmas party at Wintrell Hall. Miranda is making plans to escape a life of drudgery as a poor relation in her cousin's household, while Gerard battles bitterness that his career was cut short by the injury to his knee. However, an enemy has infiltrated the family party, bent on revenge and determined that Twelfth Night will end in someone's death …

April Kihlstrom, The Wicked Groom: When the Duke of Berenford is engaged to marry a woman he's never met, what's a poor man to do? How was he to know she wouldn't appreciate his brilliant scheme?

From Vanessa Riley, Unmasked Heart: Shy, nearsighted caregiver, Gaia Telfair never guessed she couldn't claim her father's love because of a family secret, her illicit birth. Can the mulatto passing for white survive being exposed and shunned by the powerful duke who has taken an interest in her? William St. Landon, the Duke of Cheshire, will do anything to protect his mute daughter from his late wife's scandals. He gains the help of Miss Telfair, who has the ability to help children learn to speak, but with a blackmailer at large, if only he could do a better job at shielding his heart.

Regina Scott, Secrets and Sensibilities: When art teacher Hannah Alexander accompanies her students on a country house visit, she never dreams of entering into a dalliance with the handsome new owner David Tenant. But one moment in his company and she's in danger of losing her heart, and soon her very life.

Join the Bluestocking League in celebrating the wonder of traditional Regency romance.

Vanessa Riley